Angelica put her hand on Greg's heart, feeling its wild pounding.

"Why do I feel as if you're running from me when you don't want to any more than I do?" she asked.

He held her gently. "Because you're so important to me. I can't be near you and not want more. I can't sleep knowing you're so close yet so far. I won't dishonor you by asking for more," he said. "But..."

He swallowed with difficulty. "Angel, there are so many things...things about me that I can't tell you. Not yet."

He cupped her cheek. "And I'm afraid that when I do, *you'll* be the one running."

And when that happened, he added silently, it was going to rip his heart out....

Books by Kate Welsh

Love Inspired

For the Sake of Her Child #39
Never Lie to an Angel #69

KATE WELSH

A two-time winner of Romance Writers of America's coveted Golden Heart Award, Kate lives in suburban Philadelphia with her husband of twenty-six years. She has two daughters whose childhood antics often wind up in her stories. Besides her writing career, Kate works part-time as a graphic artist and does administrative work for an international manufacturer.

As a child she was often the "scriptwriter" in neighborhood games of make-believe. Kate turned back to storytelling when her husband challenged her to write down the stories in her head. With Jesus so much a part of her life, Kate found it natural to incorporate Him into her writing. Her goal is to entertain her readers with wholesome stories of the love between two people the Lord has brought together and to teach His truths while she entertains.

Never Lie to an Angel
Kate Welsh

♥ *Love Inspired*™

Published by Steeple Hill Books™

STEEPLE HILL BOOKS

Steeple
Hill™

ISBN 0-373-87069-8

NEVER LIE TO AN ANGEL

Copyright © 1999 by Kate Welsh

Visit us at www.steeplehill.com

Printed in U.S.A.

Let all bitterness, wrath, anger, clamor, and evil
speaking be put away from you, with all malice.
And be kind to one another, tenderhearted,
forgiving one another, just as
God in Christ forgave you.

—Ephesians 4:31, 32

To the men who taught me what a hero is. Daddy, who prayed that this dream of mine would come true. You taught me that a hero can be gentle as well as strong and can lean on the One more powerful and still remain a hero. I've been blessed every day of my life to have a father like you.

And to my Uncle Bills, my godfather and my "fake" uncle, who both taught me that quiet gestures unnoticed by the many are often those remembered the longest by the few. Thanks for the memories. You are both truly missed.

Chapter One

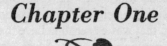

He wanted to crawl under a rock.

Watching the tiny, auburn-haired woman bustle in with a pile of clean clothes for the old man who'd come into the mission after him, gave Greg Peterson two opposite reactions at once. He longed to meet her, get to know her. And he wanted desperately to slink away unnoticed. But the latter wasn't an option. He had a job to do.

After a first glance at her, he'd spent the past two hours trying to fade into the background here. He needed to regain his equilibrium. And he hadn't yet.

Angelica DeVoe walked the stooped old man to the stairs and patted him on his rounded shoulder. He shambled his way up the steps under her watchful eye. Greg could tell how much it cost her to let him go it alone.

When her gaze swept across the room toward him, Greg felt his stomach clench. He slid a little lower in his seat, hoping she'd decide to help one of the others before getting around to him. He dropped his head back against the wall, and, with his eyes closed, prayed fervently for the first time in months. *Please, Lord, don't let her notice me yet.*

He'd come there doubting, expecting to see a pretender—a spoiled do-gooder seeking some sort of twisted glory. Or worse, he'd been ready to believe the anonymous informant who'd said drug trafficking went on inside the neighborhood mission.

For Greg, that was easier to believe than what he'd seen since arriving here two hours ago. Now, he wasn't sure what to think. And Greg hated feeling unsure.

Could one of the heirs to the DeVoe Plastics fortune give up her easy life to serve the poor of the North Riverside section of the city? Bitter past experience had taught him how unlikely that was. But now, after watching Angelica DeVoe, he had to at least allow for the possibility that the problems in this neighborhood came from another source. His own informant claimed the problems belonged on the doorstep of the Third Precinct and not on that of North Riverside Mission.

Greg hadn't wanted to believe fellow officers might be working both sides of the law for profit. He'd kept quiet about what Teddy Leach said, hoping it wasn't true because it made everything he'd gone through in the last year—bringing down one of the biggest drug operations in the city—seem in vain. It made Jessie Cushing's death pointless. It made the life he'd led for the last six years appallingly futile.

Taking a deep breath, Greg turned back to prayer. *Lord, I don't want to do this. I don't want to be here.*

Please give me wisdom, and protect the innocents caught in the middle.

"Are you all right, sir? Do you need a doctor?"

Angelica DeVoe's soft voice penetrated Greg's silent petition. He opened his eyes to find her standing in front of him, concern etched on her delicate features. He stood to show respect, and she hurriedly stepped back, leaving him embarrassed. He knew he looked like the scum of the earth.

"I was just—ah…I'm Greg Peters," he said, then stuck out his hand to shake hers. Realizing his error a split second later, he started to retract his hand, but he felt her press her hand into his.

"Welcome to North Riverside Mission," she said, her gentle green eyes staring up into his. He found the tranquility of her gaze so disquieting that he looked down and focused on her small hand engulfed in his. Greg wished again for that rock to crawl under. His hands and face were filthy, purposely dirtied as part of the setup. He was clean under his clothes, but an observer would never guess.

"Sorry," he muttered, dropping her hand and stuffing his in the pockets of his jeans. There she stood, looking like the angel on top of his parents' Christmas tree, while he looked and felt like a complete dirtbag.

He longed for a shower. Some decent clothes. A shave! A haircut. That thought gave him pause. He couldn't even remember his last shave or haircut. He'd been living on the other side too long.

"Mr. Peters, we don't get many donations for larger men. I'm not sure we have anything that will fit you. I'll certainly look, of course, but—"

"I wasn't here for a handout, Miss DeVoe. I

thought maybe you'd have something I could do around here to earn a few bucks. I'd rather earn my way.''

She blinked in surprise.

And at that Greg Peterson, reputed to be one of the toughest undercover officers in Riverside's police department, felt himself blush like a schoolboy.

''Oh,'' she said at last with a hint of a smile.

For Greg, that smile was like watching the sun burst through the clouds after a week of rain.

''You know,'' she began again, ''I've been thinking of hiring someone to fix a few things around here.''

Greg looked down at the worn toes of his beat-to-death Chuck Taylors, hoping to hide his helpless grin. Her offer meant his assignment was well on its way. He felt his grin fade as he raked a hand through his hair and remembered the petroleum jelly he'd used to make it look dirty. Right then, he wanted more than anything to look his best; instead, he looked his undercover worst.

''I'm pretty good at fixing things that are broken.'' That said, he reluctantly looked into her bottle-green eyes, and guilt seared him. ''I wouldn't be putting anyone out of a job, would I?''

Angelica DeVoe held out her small hands for his inspection. The skin was chapped and several nails were chipped and broken. Not the hands of a spoiled rich girl playing at charity. ''Oh, believe me,'' she said with a sigh, ''this is one particular job I don't mind losing. Come into my office and we'll discuss it.'' She gestured toward a door down a hall off the big main room.

Greg followed her into the small office. Like the main room, it was clean and well ordered.

"When could you start?" she asked, naming a starting salary. She raised a delicate eyebrow and gestured toward the chair in front of her desk.

Greg shrugged and sat, feeling a little like a kid called into the principal's office. "Right now, I suppose. It's not like I've got anywhere important I have to be."

"Before you sign on, there are some rules you need to know about and agree to abide by."

"I don't mind a few rules."

"My rules are simple but absolute. Break one and you're out. No excuses. No second chances. That may seem a bit rigid but North Riverside Mission has a good reputation. It has to stay that way. It's very important to our funding that anyone working here is above reproach. Rule one—no drugs. Our clinic gives monthly blood tests to make sure every resident and employee here is clean. Rule two—no alcohol on the premises, and you may not come here drunk. Rule three—no sexual misconduct on the premises. The women's dorm is, by the way, forbidden territory to all men. Rule four—every Sunday and Wednesday evening we have services. Everyone living here is expected to attend."

Greg grinned. Man oh man, that sounded good! He hadn't been able to attend services for over a year. Because he'd been so deeply undercover, he hadn't even been able to keep his Bible in the apartment he'd been using. To him, North Riverside Mission's rules were manna—

"I assure you, I'm not joking, Mr. Peters," Angelica said, considerable steel in her voice.

"I sure hope you aren't," Greg said, raking a hand through his hair again. "That was a smile of pure relief. I'd like nothing better than to attend services again. It's been too long. And it'll be nice not to have to put up with drunks and druggies. It can get real tiresome on the streets."

"You're a believer?"

"Guess I don't look the part, huh?" Greg retorted.

"I'm sorry, I just assumed you wouldn't be. Most of the people who come here have never even heard the Gospel," Angelica said, wondering at once what he was doing living on the streets. She knew from the way he stood that he was mortified by his appearance. An idea clicked in her head.

"I wonder if you might consider helping out with another problem. If you wouldn't mind cleaning out the back room, you could have it for a bedroom. I'd feel much better if someone was down here at night. There have been some threats against us from a local gang, and the police say they can't do much to protect us."

Greg Peters narrowed his startling ice-blue eyes. "What kind of threats? And who's 'us'?"

"Against me mostly, so I doubt you'd be in any danger."

"I don't really care if I am. I can take care of myself. What did they say? What kind of threats?"

Angelica felt ill just thinking of the voice on the phone. "I'd rather not repeat the things he said, if you don't mind."

"Do you know who it was? Was it personal, or related to your work here?" Greg asked.

"I'm known as something of a troublemaker in the neighborhood." She smiled. "Which doesn't bother me in the least. It tells me I'm having a positive effect. Children don't have a lot of chance to grow up to be good citizens or moral adults if they are raised in a pit of immoral behavior and violence. I'm going to save this neighborhood, Mr. Peters. One soul at a time. One household at a time."

"An admirable goal."

"You'd think the local police would think so, wouldn't you?"

"They don't?"

"They've become more a hindrance than a help. It's hard to convince people to trust the police when most of the time they're the problem."

"I don't understand. Are you saying they're crooked?"

"I'm saying they're ineffectual. And calling them appears to be a waste of time."

"What about the threats? What did the cops say about them?"

"They say they can't really do anything. No one's been hurt, and they have only my word that I've been getting calls."

"Didn't they even suggest you put caller ID on the phone?"

Angelica stared uneasily at Greg for a few seconds. How did he know so much about police work? But then she dismissed the question. Nowadays, with TV crime dramas, everyone was an armchair detective. "I'm not calling the police again until they have to admit I'm telling the truth," she told him. "That's why I want to have someone down here who can call them if anything happens. I'm not expecting heroics. In fact, I don't want any. I want those idiots over at the Third Precinct house to get here and arrest whoever it is that's threatening the mission."

"I've got it. No heroics. Just call the cops and let some thug do whatever he wants to do until the cops finally get here." His tone was calm, but his eyes glittered with anger. "Not likely, Ms. DeVoe. I may not look like a gentleman, but my mother didn't raise me to stand by and watch someone get hurt. Especially a woman."

"I meant no offense. I just wanted to keep you free of my problems—not to insult you."

Greg nodded. "No offense taken then. But I wanted you to know that if I stay here you *will* be safer. I won't turn the other cheek, or stand by and let someone get hurt."

How odd that he would be so upright and stalwart, she thought. He seemed to lack all the negative earmarks of other men in his position. "I'm sure I'll sleep better, knowing you're helping guard us at night. Now, about where you'll sleep—the store room's filled with old building materials, broken furniture and whatnot. We can have it cleared out and slap on a coat of paint by nightfall. I've got an old single dresser and a bed upstairs. It won't be much, but you'll have privacy."

"I'll clear it out myself. You must have more important things to do. You shouldn't be wasting time doing my new job."

Angelica rose. She paused, then leaned across the

desk to shake his hand. She could see that he was
embarrassed to touch her because he was so dirty.

"There are some old cans of paint in that room as
well. If you mix them all together, you'll have a liv-
able color. It should be enough to cover all the
walls."

"Yes, ma'am."

"Good. And if I don't get back before you've finished, the men's bath is on the second floor to the left
of the stairs at the back of the hall. Towels and toi-
letries are just inside on the shelf. Drop the towels off
in the laundry center at the top of the stairs."

Greg Peters stood and left with a smile on his lips.
Angelica wondered why his smile seemed so beautiful. And she wondered again why he seemed so
strong, despite his life on the streets. He was really
nothing like the men who usually came in—hooked
on drugs or liquor. Maybe that was because he was
a believer. But then, if his heart and soul were healed,
what problem was big enough to keep him on the
streets? She frowned. What had brought the man to
North Riverside Mission?

Greg straightened and stretched his back after rolling out the braided rug that Angelica had found for
his room. Hands on his hips, he surveyed his day's
work. Night's work too, he thought, exhaustion
weighing him down as he noticed that darkness had
fallen outside the small, barred window.

But it had been worth it. It felt good to labor over
something, and see tangible results. The room didn't
look half bad, either. Mixing the white, cream and

blue paint together had worked out to a pale blue
color that was easy on the eye.

Greg gave in to a yawn that stretched his jaws
wide. He was dead tired, he realized. It had taken
about two hours to haul all the junk out to the Dumpster. He shook his head and let a grin curve his lips.
He'd learned one thing. Angelica DeVoe didn't throw
out anything of the least possible value—and she kept
some stuff that didn't deserve to be called anything
but trash.

He sank to the rug and sighed. He'd shower later.
For just a few minutes, he'd close his eyes. Just to
rest them. Then he'd get up and haul the furniture in.
Just a few…minutes…

"Mr. Peters," Angelica whispered from the doorway. But her new handyman didn't move. The sun
slanted in the open window, sending a shaft of light
between them. She called his name again, a bit more
loudly—but still she got no response. Because of the
way the light bisected the room, she couldn't see him
well. Technically, if she entered his room, she'd be
breaking one of her own rules.

But he was on the floor. He might have slept there
last night, or he might have collapsed. She had no
way of knowing.

Perhaps she shouldn't have let him do so much
yesterday. Although he looked strong and healthy, his
appearance might have deceived her. Maybe he was
sick and stoically hiding it. "Greg," she called more
loudly, and stepped closer.

Greg Peters was up and in a crouch in a split second. He looked like a lion about to pounce on his

prey, and she felt momentarily like that prey. The sunlight glittered in his icy-blue eyes. He looked suddenly dangerous. Angelica jumped back, heart pounding, adrenaline surging—trying not to scream.

"I'm sorry," she said. "I'm so sorry. I was afraid you were ill. You were so still." She clenched her fists and took a deep breath.

"It's okay," he said, and stood while holding a hand up as if to implore her understanding.

"I shouldn't have startled you awake like that." Why was she making excuses? He was her employee and she had every right to wake him when he'd slept through breakfast.

"You didn't. I wake up like that sometimes. It isn't your fault. It's—uh…too many years on the street. You have to wake up fast and ready for anything. I'm sorry I frightened you."

"Startled. Not frightened," she declared, determined to believe it herself. Instinct. She understood the instinct of self-preservation. Women and even children who came to her, fleeing abusive relationships, often woke that way. Ready for anything. Ready to run. It was entirely possible that his reaction could have come from the trauma of living on the streets. She was glad that he'd wandered into her mission. Maybe here he could find a measure of the Lord's peace.

"Okay. I'm sorry I startled you then," Greg said. "Did you need me to do something for you?"

"I just noticed the furniture still in the hall and came to see if there was a problem."

"The problem is that I fell asleep on the job. I

won't let it happen again. Guess I'd better move that furniture.''

"You were still working at eleven o'clock last night, Mr. Peters. You aren't required to work twenty-four hours a day."

"Greg. Please call me Greg. Mr. Peters is—sounds like my father."

Angelica nodded. "Greg. If you fell asleep on the job, it was from exhaustion. I think you should forget moving the furniture and go on up and have your shower."

Greg got that embarrassed, wounded look in his eyes again. "I guess I'm pretty rank to be around. Sorry."

"No apology needed. And no, you aren't. But you're covered with paint." She turned to leave before she unwittingly hurt him again, but stopped and pivoted back to face him. "Oh! I almost forgot. I was wrong about there not being anything for larger men in our donations. I put a few things I think might fit you in the drawers of the dresser. I hope they're helpful."

Greg watched her rush from the room, and seconds later heard a crash. He stuck his head out in time to see the pieces of the old iron bed that Angelica had found for him falling to the floor. She made a valiant effort to control the avalanche, but it was beyond her. With a self-deprecating laugh, she stood in the midst of the destruction. "Oops," she said with a little shrug.

"I'll get it. Don't try to—"

But he spoke too late. She'd already hefted the bed rail up to lean it against the wall where it had been.

She neatly hooked the cord of the old brass floor lamp, and as she lifted the end of the bed rail upward, the lamp started to topple. Greg made a grab for it and caught it, but the ruckus wasn't over yet.

When Angelica tried to untangle the cord from the hooked end of the bed rail, she bumped into the mattress. The mattress started to sag over at the top, so the dresser in front of it began to teeter. Greg dropped the lamp and threw his body into the mattress just in time, but at the same time Angelica also tried to stop the mattress's curling descent. Bedrail still in hand, she thrust out her arms to stop it. That destabilized the mattress more, and it and the dresser fell over. The heavy iron bed rail conked Greg over the head. Then it hooked into the tear in the shoulder of his shirt and ripped the old material leaving him with only half a shirt front, just as Angelica disappeared under the mattress.

Tearing fabric was the last sound to be heard in the hall.

Then Greg heard a surprising, unladylike snicker leak out from under the flowered mattress. A chuckle rose to follow it. Then laughter began and kept rolling out from under the load of upholstered stuffing.

"Are you all right?" he asked. He went to lift the mattress, but thought better of it. "Don't move. Don't help. Please just stay where you are and let me take care of this. Okay?"

She laughed harder, and Greg felt a chuckle of his own rise to the surface. He was laughing as hard as she was by the time he'd stood the mattress up and righted the dresser. Tears rolled down his face, and he leaned against the wall and held his laughter-sore stomach.

Then he realized that she was simply staring at him. No, not at him—at his chest. He too glanced down—and understood. She was staring at the angry red scar from the bullet he'd taken two months earlier when he'd tried to pull his partner to safety. He searched for a way to explain it without lying.

"You were shot," she said, her eyes wide and wary. "Who shot you?"

"I got caught in a cross fire. When I woke up in the hospital, they told me a drug deal had gone bad, and that the gunman had started shooting like a wild man. Like I said, sometimes it gets rough on the streets."

"Why do you live down here the way you do?"

"Some of us don't have a choice," he snapped. "Why don't you tell me? Why do you do it?"

Greg didn't wait for an answer, but stalked down the hall, through the kitchen and outside—more angry at himself than at Angelica. It wasn't her fault he was there. The captain should have let him take a long vacation. Instead, he'd followed up two weeks in the hospital and six weeks recuperating with an assignment they briefed him on while he was still flat on his back. And that assignment had put him here, back on the streets.

Outside, he sank down on the back steps that overlooked the playground. A couple of teens were shooting hoops on the ball court, and off to the side, behind a ten-foot chain-link fence, three small kids swung on the old swings. A guy walked in the gate from the street and across the blacktop. He stood for a time, watching the game of one-on-one, and then said something to the teens that Greg was too far away to hear.

He wore a black T-shirt, drooping black pants and a backward baseball cap. Greg guessed his age to be nearly the same as that of the ball players. The teens made no secret that they wanted him to leave. He persisted, and the two boys walked away to push the little kids on the swing. Black T followed. The teen with the basketball threw it at him and shouted something.

Greg had seen enough.

When the young guy saw Greg approach, he turned to leave. He hesitated, watching Greg, clearly unsure whether to run or act cool. He settled on backing up toward the gate, but he finally realized that he didn't have a chance. So he turned and stood his ground. Greg knew the type. He'd probably be real brave in a crowd. "So, what'ya sellin'?" Greg asked quickly.

Black T looked him over. "Who's askin'?"

"A potential customer," Greg answered.

"What kind of potential?" Black T asked.

"The buying kind." Greg stared at him knowingly, intently. "But we don't meet here, and you don't try selling to the North Riverside Mission kids again."

"Why should you care who I sell to?"

Greg narrowed his eyes and yanked the guy closer by his shirt. "I care that you don't tip off the dragon lady to my habits," he snarled. "I've got a good thing going here. Free room and board and cash, and all for handling a few odd jobs. So is it a deal? You weren't getting anywhere with those kids anyway."

Black T reached up and pried Greg's fingers loose.

Greg let him. The dealer stepped away, rubbing his palms on his baggy pants. "Yeah. Yeah, dude, it's a deal. I can get most anything you'd want."

"Give me your cell phone number. I'll call when I need a score and tell you what I'm looking for."

Information exchanged, Black T took off. Greg looked back toward the old school-building-turned-neighborhood-mission. Black T hadn't seemed shocked that he wasn't wanted on the playground. That was good. If Angelica DeVoe were the connection, she wouldn't care about drug sales to her kids. But then again, he told himself, she would want such activities kept away from her. There was nothing to do but search the building. Now he just had to come up with a way to search a large building without tipping anyone off.

After a while he returned to the building to move the furniture, but he found the hall empty. Someone had moved all the furniture in, put curtains on the window and even made the bed with a matching spread. Everything was worn, but made the room feel more like home than his own place.

Angelica DeVoe was a mystery. Just when he had her pegged as all business, she threw him a curve, laughing or performing some kindness.

The clothes were indeed his size. He remembered the knapsack he'd left under the bench in the main room. He'd stuffed another pair of torn jeans and a shirt in it. She must have checked the sizes and acquired clothes for him.

He didn't need this. Guilt over Jessie's death still kept him awake at night, and memories of holding his partner as she died still woke him when he did manage to sleep. He didn't need guilt for taking charity from Angelica when some other person in North Riverside needed her help more.

He just didn't need any more guilt.

Chapter Two

"Please sit down," Angelica said when Greg entered her office. She didn't look up, but took a few more seconds, hoping to calm down. Bad timing had placed Greg at her office door seconds after her phone call from Harold Whiting. She wished she had more time to examine why Greg's duplicity angered her to the degree it did. Perhaps because she'd had high hopes for his rehabilitation.

When she looked up, it was to a view of the top of Greg's head. He seemed to be studying a tablet on his lap. Surprised by how light his hair was now that it was clean, she noticed that even though it hung in loose waves to his shoulders, the length seemed to emphasize his masculinity rather than detract from it. The fact that she'd noticed anything at all about his physical attributes angered her all the more. This man had lied to her, and that was one thing she didn't—couldn't—tolerate.

"I'll get right to the point, Mr. Peters. I don't like being lied to."

Greg's head snapped up and—if she read his face correctly—his expression was riddled with guilt. "Lied to? What makes you think I've lied to you?"

"You were seen talking to a gang member this morning, one of the Judges. He's a known pusher. I told you that anyone on staff has to be above reproach. I told you there were no second chances with me. I meant it. Associating with members of the gang threatening the mission isn't what I had in mind when I offered you a place to live and work. I cannot allow you to jeopardize our funding. It wasn't just a resident or a neighbor who saw you earlier. It was a trustee."

"Then it's your policy to open your playground to pushers?"

"Of course not!"

"Did you bother to ask the kids about what happened?" he demanded.

"I just got off the phone with the trustee. I didn't know anyone else was involved. I'll have to—"

"Did your trustee happen to mention," Greg cut in, his eyes a burning blue, "that they'd already told the guy to get lost and had walked away from him? Did he say that the bum followed those kids over to the tot lot where there were some little ones playing? Or that the strung-out little weasel lit out of there like a shot after I told him not to come on mission property again?"

"He didn't say a thing about seeing anyone else, or that there were boys being solicited. I—" Angelica closed her eyes for a few seconds and rested her head on the high back of her chair, then she sat forward and met his gaze. "He also didn't mention that the talk you and the pusher were engaged in was a confrontation. I jumped to the same conclusions he did. My only defense is that he was threatening to pull his funding and the loss of even one large donor like him would put us under. But that's no excuse. I sincerely apologize, Greg."

"How'd this trustee know the weasel was one of the Judges?"

While he maintained a neutral mien, giving away none of his thoughts, she was sure she'd heard suspicion in Greg's tone. That was as puzzling as the guilt that she was sure she'd read in his eyes when she'd accused him of lying.

"The trustee who called is Harold Whiting, the local district judge. That weasel, as you called him, and several more of his gang, have managed to squeeze through Harold's court on technicalities—mistakes made by those idiots at the Third Precinct. In case you didn't get the correlation, the baggy black T-shirts and pants are practically a uniform for the gang, and meant to mock a judge's robes. The Judges are a particularly annoying thorn in Harold's side."

"I'll bet."

"I'm truly sorry about the mistake, but this does illustrate what I said yesterday about us being above reproach. I'll smooth things over with Harold. Don't worry about this."

Greg stood and glanced down at the tablet he held. "Don't worry about what?"

"The incident. It's over. Again, I'm truly sorry."

"Sounds as if you were only given half the facts,

so no problem. But what would I have to worry about?''

"Harold is a bit—excitable. He wanted me to fire you.''

Greg's head tilted and he considered her with narrowed eyes for a second. "And you were firing me when I first came in here?''

"I hoped you'd have an explanation, but, truthfully, I didn't think you would. Kicking a drug habit is difficult—some claim impossible. I believe Christ can heal addictions of all kinds, or I wouldn't be here. But even He's no guarantee against temptation if someone turns away from His help.''

"And you figured I had. That I was an addict. Or that I lied about my faith.'' Angelica heard anger lace his voice now, and she couldn't blame him. Being doubted about your abilities was one thing, but being doubted about your commitment to the Lord was another thing altogether.

"I'm sorry, but, yes, that's exactly what I thought. Perhaps Harold didn't see what happened from a neutral position. He may have judged you on your appearance. I *will* speak to him. Believe me.''

Greg tried to tamp down his anger, but it flared nonetheless. "Thanks for your faith in me. I'll pack—'' He broke off, something stronger than his anger shutting off his words. Pulling out of this assignment would be a stupid, grandstand play, and it would hurt a lot of people. Drugs were pouring into North Riverside at an alarming rate. It had to stop. He stared up at the ceiling and prayed for clarity of thought.

He had to admit to himself that she'd been given

essentially the right information about what had gone down out on that playground. He'd made sure that it looked like a confrontation and that the pusher wouldn't be back, but he *had* been setting up a buy. Still, he felt betrayed—which was ridiculous. After all, he was in the middle of searching her mission for drugs on the pretense of reviewing needed repairs. He'd been judged more or less accurately, while she was a suspect despite all outward signs that there was no way she would be involved in drug trafficking. Talk about casting the first stone!

Ashamed, Greg grimaced. "No," he said into the tense silence. "I won't pack. I need this job. I need to help out here, and I need to convince you that I'm not what I look like. I'm not even sure why I need that, but I do."

Angelica smiled slightly and her eyes softened. "Then I'm glad you've decided to stay. I'm sure you'll be an asset here at North Riverside Mission."

"Count on it," Greg said, then left. He got halfway down the short hall when he remembered why he'd gone to her office. He'd wanted to discuss some of the needed repairs that he'd already identified, and he needed permission to venture onto the forbidden sections of the third floor.

"I wish you'd told me the whole story, Harold!" Greg heard Angelica declare, evidently back on the phone. He couldn't believe the anger in her voice. This was her precious trustee, and she was angry on Greg's account. She was risking her funding to stick up for him.

Guilt warred with pleasure. He listened spellbound as she explained his actions. Thinking he should leave, he turned, but stopped in amazement as Angelica began defending even his hair.

"No, I will *not* tell him to shave his beard and cut his hair. Long hair and beards are not immoral, Harold. Men in Jesus's time probably looked more like Greg Peters than you do. He professes to know Christ, and until I see otherwise, he will remain here. If the Judges decided to come to a service, I couldn't turn them away.

"As I recall, Harold, you were elected by a landslide last election—a landslide that was largely due to the record voter turnout from this district. They felt you had shown a genuine interest in them through your support of this mission.

"Perhaps if you attended services with us once in a while, you'd get a better feel for the Spirit that surrounds North Riverside." Greg could hear the softness return to her voice as she spoke of the Spirit. Apparently Harold Whiting did, too, for Angelica said, "I'll certainly look forward to seeing you and your wife on Sunday night. Yes, seven-thirty. See you then. And God Bless."

Greg heard Angelica release a gusty sigh as she dropped the receiver in the cradle. He smiled, but he really wanted to applaud; maybe she was getting past his appearance. His smile faded, and he turned away and leaned against the wall, staring at the tablet.

Why did he care what she thought of him? Nothing could come of their acquaintance. He was still lying to her—still using her and her mission. And it seemed his activities had already jeopardized at least part of her funding, and would continue to do so until the drug leak in this part of the city was plugged. If she was the drug connection, he would shut the mission down, and she'd go to prison. Of course, he'd begun to doubt that scenario five minutes after walking in here. It was more likely a number of Third Precinct cops. And every drug buy he made to trap his fellow officers would put North Riverside Mission and her funding at risk.

"Greg? Was there something else? It occurred to me that you must have come to my office for a reason."

Greg turned to face her. She stood just outside her office, and rays of sunlight streamed in the high, tall windows of the hall. Her auburn hair seemed aflame. So lovely, he thought vaguely. "I need to check the third floor and roof to see what needs doing. I thought we could meet after that and prioritize the list."

"What have you found so far?" she asked, pointing to his tablet.

"Nothing," Greg said, trying to tear his eyes from her face and resist the sheer pull of her. She just couldn't turn out to be the problem. No one this angelic could poison the lives of the very people she purported to want to save. And it wasn't just that she was pretty. She was—but there was a beauty inside her that shone in her eyes and her gentle smile. She was a tough lady with a heart of gold.

"Nothing?" she asked, happily incredulous.

Her tone snapped him out of his reverie. "Nothing *upsetting,* I mean." He grinned. "There are lots of things that need tending."

"Oh," she sighed. "From the heights to the depths. How bad is it?"

"They're things I can do myself so it's not too bad.

I do need to look at the third floor though,'' he added, mentioning the area that had been off limits.

"Oh sure. That's fine,'' she replied easily. "I've been worried. I just haven't had time to see to everything that needs fixing. I'm glad the Lord sent you here.''

Her relieved smile put one more nail in the coffin of the Third Precinct. She obviously had nothing to hide on the third floor, and if she had the money to make costly repairs, she'd have had them done—not worried over how bad it had gotten. He wished she wasn't so grateful that he was there to do the repairs; that made him feel guiltier for even being here. And he knew she'd change her mind when she found out who he really was.

It was sunset when Greg finished on the roof. He'd checked the entire building, top to bottom. His list of repairs was compiled, and he was sure there were no drugs filtering through North Riverside Mission. He'd done a thorough search under the guise of checking every nook and cranny for problems that needed work.

He'd even used the passkey to check Angelica's apartment. While decorated with taste and style, nothing had pointed to her wealthy background, let alone a large income from drug sales.

At first glance, the furnishings looked like antiques—but he knew antiques. He had learned them, watching his mother run her small antique shop. No, Angelica's treasures were crafty flea market finds circa 1930 or 1940, and carefully repaired.

Her closet wasn't full, and the clothes she had,

while expensive, weren't new. Most, he'd say, were several years old. Her reading material ran toward Christian commentaries and inspirational fiction. She wasn't spending illegal income on opulent living, and he already knew her bank account had passed muster.

As far as he was concerned, she was in the clear.

And the Third Precinct cops looked more guilty by the hour. From the roof, he watched and snapped a few pictures of drug buys. Watching over the front wall, Greg spied pushers, working three different street corners of Rockland Street, checking their watches, then heading indoors just as a patrol car turned the corner onto the street. Because of the size of the old school building and its grounds, Greg was able to watch the patrol car navigate the entire block. The pattern repeated itself on all four streets. The Judges knew the patrol schedule.

Of course, that only proved what Angelica had charged—that the Precinct cops were incompetent. But inner-city cops couldn't be naive enough to establish predictable rounds, and it was also against regulations. Still he needed more than Teddy Leach's questionable word.

Just as the patrol car passed out of Greg's line of sight, he heard shouting from the front of the building. A tree blocked Greg's view, but he could hear kids crying. A woman's scream rushed up at him, and a man's voice raised in anger. Then a softer sound, a calmer voice.

Angelica.

Greg pivoted and bolted for the door to the building. All he could think was that he'd promised to protect her and that she'd been counting on him. He circled the building from back to front, hoping to add an element of surprise.

Greg rounded the corner on silent feet. The scene before him made his heart skip a beat. A man in black—the Judges' uniform—staggered up to the top of the steps, where Angelica stood protectively in front of a woman and two children. The woman looked scared and as if she'd been roughed up. Greg didn't have a clear look at the kids.

"Please, Mr. Jackson," Angelica said, her voice soothing and calm, "let Mary and the children go inside, and you and I will sit down out here and talk this over." Greg could see her in profile. She was about twelve feet from Jackson—within striking distance if the guy wanted to hit another woman. From the look of his balled fists, Greg figured he just might.

"Talk," Jackson snarled. "That's all you women want to do—talk. I'm sick of talking. I want her and them kids to get home, and now!"

"What you're doing to Mary is wrong, and deep down you know that."

"She's mine and I'll treat her any way I want. She's supposed to obey me. Your Bible says that. I remember."

"It also says that husbands should love their wives as Christ loves His church. He laid down His life for His church, Mr. Jackson."

He staggered and shouted, "They're mine and I can do what I want with them!"

Greg had heard enough. Bullies and abusers were about as low as a man could get, as far as Greg was concerned, and this one wasn't even a little repentant. Greg knew he had to act before things went any further. He moved from the cover of the building to a tree. There was a short wall about ten feet from the tree that he could use as cover. He shot across the open space and dove behind the wall.

"Sam. It is Sam, isn't it?" Angelica asked.

"Yeah, that's my name," Jackson said, sounding a bit calmer. Angelica's tone never lost its soothing cadence, but Greg's heart rate doubled because as he peered over the wall, Jackson moved a couple of feet closer to her.

"Sam, your wife loves you," Angelica said, her voice still measured, still soothing. "You don't really want to hurt her, do you?"

"She don't listen to me no more."

Greg inched along the ground behind the wall and got to his feet directly behind Sam Jackson at the bottom of the stairs. Maybe this much caution wasn't necessary, but this was one of the Judges, and he might have a weapon within reach. Once at the top, Greg knew he'd only have a second or two to surprise the guy to take him down without a struggle.

He knew Angelica saw him, but, thankfully, she didn't react. She just kept talking, trying to distract Jackson, who moved yet another couple of feet closer to her.

"Sam, you can't expect any good to come of acting this way."

"Good? What good she ever done me?"

"She gave you her love and two beautiful children."

That apparently gave Jackson something to think about, and Greg was grateful. Because it went down like most police work. Lots of careful planning, then a quick flurry of activity. Greg crept up the last three steps, hoping his own reflection didn't give him away. When he was right behind Jackson, he brought his hands up from behind and pulled the guy's arms behind his back. They tussled for a couple of seconds, then Greg had him on the ground and subdued.

"Call the cops," he shouted to a woman who stepped outside behind Angelica. Mrs. Jackson and her children were already wrapped in Angelica's embrace.

"No," Mary Jackson protested. "He's been crazy for weeks since he lost his job."

Greg shook his head. Why did they always try to protect their abusive husbands? Sam Jackson struggled in Greg's hold then, growling. Greg looked up into the woman's eyes. "He's not going to change, ma'am. You've got no choice here. You've got those kids to protect." To Angelica, he said, "Why don't you take Mrs. Jackson and her kids inside to wait for the police. Maybe you could explain to her why she has to press charges."

Five minutes later—far too long, Greg thought, considering that the station house was three blocks away—a cruiser pulled up, and two swaggering patrolmen got out. In seconds, he heard the unmistakable sound of police specials being pulled and cocked.

"You, there. Step back and put your hands up."

Greg looked over his shoulder. "Me? This is the perp—person you were called about. He hurt his wife and was trying to force her to go home with him. I stopped him."

Sam Jackson started screaming, charging that Greg had assaulted him. And he started to struggle again.

The cops grabbed Greg and pulled him off Jackson over the protests of several North Riverside witnesses. The two cops held Greg, as Jackson scrambled to his feet.

Greg saw a fist fly toward him. He flinched to the left and avoided being hit. At the same time, one of the two cops let go and ducked Jackson's fist. Greg twisted away, but he overbalanced and fell against an iron post left over from a long-gone railing. He hissed as the pole tore through his shirt and scraped his side. The cop who still held on, dropped Greg's arm and jumped out of the way when Jackson swung again. The two cops, finally having figured out who they were there to arrest, wrestled Jackson to the ground. In minutes, Sam Jackson was cuffed and in the back of the patrol car.

Greg, meanwhile, sank down on the second step, strangely light-headed. He looked at his watch, surprised that only ten minutes had gone by since he'd stood on the roof and first heard voices raised in anger.

"Hey, buddy. Sorry for the mistake," one of the cops said.

"I tried to tell you."

"Yeah, but look at it from our side."

Greg read the name on the badge. John Worth. He'd remember. "Your side?" he asked.

"Yeah, we pull up, and there's Mr. Straight-and-Narrow laid out under your knee, and there's you looking like somebody out of a back alley. What were we supposed to think?"

Greg longed to ask him if he'd slept through the Academy. Instead, he said, "First, you should have made sure who was telling the truth and not judged by personal prejudice. He wasn't in any danger, or a danger to anyone else—until you two clods turned him loose. Second, you both need your eyes examined. Mr. Straight-and-Narrow there is one of the Judges. You know, baggy black pants and black T? Their uniform!''

''You just about done ranting, pal?'' the second patrolman asked, ignoring Greg's mention of the local gang.

''Just about,'' Greg replied as he shifted his gaze to the other man. Bob Gates, he read on the name tag above his badge. Another name to remember.

Gates pointed to Greg's side. ''You pressing charges?''

Greg, whose adrenaline rush was just subsiding, looked at his side. He hadn't even noticed that he was bleeding. No wonder he was light-headed. It was an annoying reaction he had to nearly any blood loss. ''Oh, man. I liked this shirt,'' he said absently, checking his bleeding side through the tear left by the post. His mind went off in a different direction, however.

He was thinking that the Lord sure worked in strange ways. He could now press assault charges. After all, the guy had come at him in front of about twenty witnesses. Considering the guy's ties to the Judges, Jackson was more dangerous than the average spousal abuser. And it seemed that his wife was going to be safe from ol' Sam, whether she had the nerve to press charges or not. His only worry about testifying concerned his cover, but he figured that he'd be done with his assignment before the preliminary hearing even came up.

"Yeah," he said. "I'm gonna press charges. The guy's a loose cannon. With the assault on his wife, you'll have him on two counts."

"You sound like you know an awful lot about police work," Gates said.

"Love those police shows on TV. Never miss them," Greg quipped.

"So you work here?" Gates asked.

"Yeah." He glanced back when the door to the mission pushed open.

Angelica DeVoe strode out like a miniature avenging angel, stood surveying the scene for a few seconds, then stalked toward them. "Mrs. Jackson has agreed to press charges. The mission's lawyer will bring her around. I don't want what happened the last time Sam Jackson went on a rampage to happen again. Have you read him his rights?"

Worth and Gates looked at each other. "He's drunk as a skunk," Worth said. "He wouldn't understand a thing we said. It'd be a waste of time, Ms. DeVoe."

Greg opened his mouth to tell them to read Jackson his Miranda warnings anyway, but Angelica did it for him. Then she walked down to the car to witness them doing it. She asked Jackson if he understood what they'd said. She advised him not to say anything until his court-appointed attorney arrived.

Worth and Gates were clearly furious, and it was easy to see why someone from the Precinct had tried to set her up as a suspect. If the word ever got out that she was being investigated, her funding would collapse like a house of cards before the charges could be disproved. And that would take one red-headed angel out of their hair. It all made perfect sense, but

Greg still feared there was more—much more—than incompetence or even bribery going on at the Third.

Still light-headed, Greg sat where he was. He wasn't about to stand just so he could fall back down. His side burned like fire now, but still he waited. The patrol car left with Jackson in the back; the crowd drifted back inside or off to their homes; the lawyer arrived and took Mrs. Jackson to the station.

Finally, Angelica came back outside and sat down on the top step next to him.

"Thank you. I think what you did and said may have changed that woman's life," she said. "I don't think any man has ever defended her. You surprised me. I didn't think anyone as big as you could move so silently. Were you in the service?"

"I was a Boy Scout. Does that count?" he answered, and smiled up at her with effort. He wished she'd leave so he could grab someone to help him inside.

Angelica had to stifle a gasp when she saw him smile. He was incredibly handsome. His eyes were beautiful when they sparkled with mirth, but it was that smile of his that changed his face and, in spite of his rather scruffy beard, made him look boyish and sensual all at the same time.

He affected her in a way no other man ever had. And that was a problem. More and more, she wondered about his story. What circumstances had brought him to the mission? He seemed honest, intelligent, reliable and hardworking. And now, she had to add "bravery" to the list of fine qualities. But, he was her employee. And she had no business being attracted to an employee, no matter how captivating he was. But her feelings were not his fault. He deserved her help as much as any of the other people who came through North Riverside Mission. And he showed such promise. She felt sure that all it would take was prayer, a little guidance, and maybe a few heart-to-heart talks, and Greg would be on the road back to being a productive member of society and a credit to the Lord.

Chapter Three

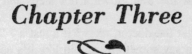

Angelica needed a little time away from Greg to get her feelings under control, especially if she was going to help him in spite of her attraction to him. "Well," she said as she stood, "I've got a mountain of paperwork waiting. Bill collectors wait for no man. Or God, it would seem. Perhaps we could put off that meeting until sometime tomorrow?"

"Yeah, sure. That'd be fine," Greg said, and stood as she did. But he paled instantly and swayed on his feet.

She was on the top step and he was on the second, so it was impossible for her to miss the disorientation that flooded his gaze.

"Uh...Miss DeVoe, is that doctor still here?" he asked and reached out for her, grasping her upper arms to steady himself.

"What is it? What's wrong?" Angelica asked.

"It's nothing really. Just a scrape," he said, as if that clarified everything.

"A scrape? A scrape from what? Where?"

"My side. From the tussle with Jackson."

"Sit," Angelica ordered. She would have felt better if he'd argued. But instead of refusing, which was more or less what she expected, gratitude flashed across his face. Then he let go of her and eased back down onto the top step. "Now, let me see," she demanded as she went down a few steps and turned to face him.

"Just get the doctor, okay? It's just a—"

"If you say something stupid like it's only a flesh wound, I swear I'll scream. What possessed you to sit here all this time chatting with neighbors and not telling anyone you were hurt?"

"I wasn't hurt. It's really just a scratch from that broken railing."

Angelica carefully lifted his shirt. Her first thought was that there was a lot of blood for a scratch. But it was a gash. A three-inch-long gash that would need stitches.

"This isn't what I hired you for," she said with pretended crossness. "I told you I didn't want you to get hurt, remember?"

Greg chuckled. "Guess I forgot. Sorry."

Angelica looked up at the front doors as the cook came out. "Emanuel, would you get Dr. Satie. Mr. Peters has been injured."

"Manny," Greg called over his shoulder. "Give me a hand here. We'll tell the doc together. No offense," he told Angelica, "but Manny's a little better equipped to catch me if I fall, and I've got to get inside eventually. I've been waiting to feel better, but it's not happening."

She smiled. "I understand." Then, leaving him to Manny's tender mercies, Angelica raced ahead to tell Dr. Dora Satie that she had a patient.

"I have no nurse. She left just minutes ago," the young Indian woman told her. "You must please stay to help."

Angelica readily agreed, thinking she'd have stayed anyway. Greg had looked so pale, and his injuries were her fault.

"This is really embarrassing," he told Manny the cook and another resident as they steered him into the small treatment room. He was pale as death and breathing oddly.

He's in worse shape than I realized, Angelica thought, as Dr. Satie broke a vial of smelling salts under his nose.

"I hate that stuff," he grumbled, turning his head.

Dr. Satie chuckled and helped him off with his shirt. "You will need stitches. I am not yet sure how many."

Greg shook his head. "Just tape it."

"Stitches," Dr. Satie countered.

"Tape," Greg declared.

Angelica felt like a spectator at a tennis match. "Greg, Dr. Satie knows what she's doing."

Greg started to get off the table, but Angelica stepped forward and pushed him back. It was pathetic how easily he sank down to the table. "Are you afraid of stitches?"

"Of course not," he snapped.

But she could tell that he was, which made her smile. He'd fearlessly faced a drunken, enraged bull of a man, but now he was afraid of a four-foot-eleven-

inch female doctor and her needle and thread. Angelica's smile faded as her gaze locked with his. She
took his hands and guided him down to lie on his
uninjured side, then sat on a stool at the head of the
table. "I'll hold your hands. It'll all be over in a few
minutes."

Greg smiled faintly. "No, it won't. But that's okay.
Mrs. Jackson's safe," he said, his gaze grabbing hold
of hers and not letting go, while the doctor stitched
his wound closed. Angelica was shaken to her core
by the connection she felt with him. It was as if a
bond had been forged between them out on those
steps in those desperate moments when futures had
hung in the balance. These moments together were
further cementing that bond.

Angelica was increasingly unsure that she could
keep her feelings out of their relationship, but she was
determined to try in order not to shortchange Greg.
He deserved her help. And he would have it.

Greg strolled through the main room of the mission. He sidestepped a little girl chasing a ball, and
grinned as the day-care worker herded the little ones
off toward the dining hall. There were kids everywhere he went. Today's rain had swelled the volume
of children at the mission to the overrun mark, but it
lent an exuberance to the atmosphere that Greg found
oddly restful. When children were happy, it was so
easy to believe that all was well with the world.

He glanced up at the big old clock over the front
doors, and picked up his pace. He'd overslept, thanks
to another night of bad dreams interspersed with per-
iods when his side had throbbed painfully. So now he

was late for his meeting with Angelica to go over his list of building repairs.

Greg had just reached her door when he heard her talking to someone. Then her words and the agitated tone in her voice registered in his groggy brain.

"I—I wish you'd stop calling me like this. I'm not going to pack up and desert North Riverside, no matter how vile your language or how preposterous your threats. I'm helping the people here. I'm doing the Lord's work."

Then he heard the unmistakable sound of a receiver slamming into a cradle. Greg knocked, but didn't wait for an invitation to enter. "You okay?" he asked, peering around the door.

Angelica stood behind her desk, staring down at the telephone. She looked up at him and smiled, but it was clearly such an effort that she gave up the charade after a couple of seconds. "It's nothing. Just a crank call."

Skeptical, Greg arched an eyebrow. "Sounded a little more serious than that."

Angelica dropped into her desk chair. As she put her hand to her forehead, Greg noticed the hand was shaking. He stalked to the desk, lifted the receiver and hit star-69. It rang, but a local cell phone provider's recording came on, saying that the cell phone was from out of the service area. It was a common trick lawbreakers used—to have a phone from another area code, which made tracing calls difficult. Greg slammed the phone back down and sat on the corner of the desk.

"Was it the same guy who threatened you before?"

Angelica nodded. "I think so."

"What did he say?"

"Nothing I'd care to repeat, and a few words I don't know the meaning of. Nor do I wish to."

"Was that all it was—an obscene phone call? Or were there threats you didn't understand, too?"

"Those, I understood. He said they weren't going to give me a minute's peace and—" Her voice cracked.

"And?" Greg coaxed.

"And that they were coming to get me. It's silly—I'm never alone except at night in my apartment. We lock the doors at midnight, and there are bars on all the ground-floor windows."

Her emerging offhandedness irritated him. "And you aren't scared?" he asked, knowing she was.

Angelica straightened her spine, sitting a little straighter. "They aren't going to stop me. They can't. I can't let them. I'm going to keep on with my work here. Besides, they're just idle threats—probably a few juvenile delinquents. They need to see that I'm not intimidated by them."

"They need a good swift kick," he growled.

"Greg, we have to treat these troubled teenagers with love. I'm hoping eventually they'll see how much better life would be for them outside the gang."

"Then you're sure it was one of the Judges?"

"They haven't really made a secret of the fact that I bother them. But don't you see? Often people who get the angriest when presented with the Gospel are the ones the message is reaching. They see that they're wrong and don't want to face it."

"Angelica, these kids aren't listening to you. All

they see is that every drug addict you turn on to Jesus and off drugs is one less customer. They understand the very basic fact that as your message reaches the adults, they become less tolerant of drugs being sold in front of their houses. They know that if you succeed, they fail.''

Angelica twirled around in her chair, then stood, facing him from the other side of the desk. "I'm not blind. I see that. But I won't write them off, either."

Greg couldn't help but smile. She was wonderful. A fool—but a wonderful one. He'd just have to watch out for her, since she refused to do it herself.

The first "accident" happened just after dinner was served. Angelica had just sat down next to Greg, when Manny shouted from the kitchen that the Dumpster out behind the mission was on fire. Greg leaped up, and groaned as he pulled the stitches. He ran full tilt toward the rear entrance, ignoring the pain.

"Close the windows before the place is full of smoke," he called to Angelica, who was right on his heels. When he joined Manny, the cook was about to throw back the lid of the Dumpster, wearing his big oven mitts as protection.

"Don't!" Greg shouted. "The flames'll surge right into your face."

He grabbed a broom and tossed it to Manny so he could use the handle to push the lid up. Greg got ready with the garden hose. As soon as Manny pried the cover open, Greg flooded the Dumpster with water. The blaze sputtered out in seconds.

When Greg turned toward the mission, the residents were all standing on the steps. They applauded, and for the first time since arriving at the mission, Greg was glad of the beard and wild hair. It would hide the blush that he felt darken his face.

Angelica rushed across the space between them. "That was such quick thinking. You were wonderful."

"Just common sense," he contended. "Let's all get back to Manny's Heavenly Hamburger." Greg took Angelica's elbow and steered her toward the back steps. "And Manny," he called over his shoulder with a teasing grin, "try not to set the trash on fire again until we get finished."

"Yeah. Right, Peters. Don't worry. *I* won't."

Greg stopped when he heard the emphasis that the cook put on *I*. Dropping Angelica's arm, he pivoted back to face Manny.

"Greg, aren't you going to eat now? It's a dish that needs to be eaten hot," Angelica said.

"I'll be along in a minute," he said. "I just want to make sure the fire's completely out." When Angelica was out of earshot, Greg walked back toward the cook. "Manny, was there something funny with the way this thing started?"

"Don't have a clue how it started. But I'm careful what I toss in there, since this happened before. It's those punks, I tell you. Those punks in black."

"The Judges? You think they started this?"

"Nothing I tossed in there could start a fire. I'd bet a month's pay on it—if I still gambled, that is."

"Let's get together out here a little later and see if we can figure out what started this."

"Sure thing," Manny said with a swing of the

broom. It came to rest across his shoulder, and he started off for the back door of the mission.

Two hours later, just as the sun set, Greg found the flare that had set the Dumpster burning. As he and Manny tossed the trash back in the big container, Greg considered their next move. Manny was thinking along the same lines, and finally asked, "So do we call the cops?"

"Think it'll do any good?"

"Nope. If you ask me, those cops and the Judges are just too cozy. This was a nice place to live when I came here. I've watched this neighborhood fall apart in about five years. The cops just sat back and gave the streets to the bad guys."

"That's just about what I thought." It went against everything he'd always believed about the law, but he had to admit that calling the police—at least the Third Precinct police—would be a mistake. "Maybe what we need to do is *not* call them. That way they won't know they're getting to Angelica. Suppose we just keep a sharp eye out for trouble. She had a nasty call earlier today, and this could just be a start."

"Will do," Manny said, and disappeared into the rising fog.

Greg checked his watch. He had about fifteen minutes until he met his "connection." Greg couldn't wait to testify against the little weasel. That was the part of Greg's job that he liked best. Testifying. Putting one more supplier of death behind bars.

It was why he'd become a cop—why he did this. It was why he couldn't stop.

His brother was still dead. He'd still missed the signs of drug abuse that one brother sharing a room with another should have seen. But maybe if he kept at it someone else's brother would never be asked that first time if he wanted to get high. And maybe some other brother wouldn't stand at his sibling's grave, wishing it was him instead, cold in the box being lowered into the ground.

Greg shook his head and walked off into the thickening fog. It was a perfect night for undercover work. His own father wouldn't even recognize him in this soup.

Outside the closet on the second floor near the children's dorm, Angelica stood, trying to console the frightened child on the other side of the door. "Try not to cry, Gina. You'll have an asthma attack. I'll find Mr. Greg. He'll have you out in no time. I'll be right back."

She found him on the first floor, tossing tools in his work caddy. "You promised me that you'd take it easy," she said. When he looked up from wiping off a wrench, a wry grin curving his lips and his blue eyes glinting with humor, every thought flew out of Angelica's head. She could only stare.

"Fixing a leaky faucet *is* easy," he explained, and chuckled.

"Oh," she replied, then suddenly remembered that while she stood staring dumbly at him, a small child was trapped in a dark closet.

"It's Gina. She shut herself in the big walk-in closet on the second floor. It's locked. I tried but I can't get it open. She's crying. I'm afraid she'll have an asthma attack if she gets much more upset."

When they arrived back upstairs, Gina's pitiful

sobs and labored breathing wafted through the heavy door.

Greg frowned down at the locked doorknob. "I know I checked this out my first day here. It was in good working order. Gina, sweetheart," he said, "can you reach the light next to the door?" Gina cried harder—gasped harder.

"I tried that with her already. The bulb seems to have burned out," Angelica answered.

Greg didn't comment, but he looked troubled as he hunkered down next to the door to check the lock. He started talking to Gina through the door, gentling her with promises and stories. The sobs slowed, as did her wheezing, as he chatted on about how he'd gotten locked in a closet when he was young.

"Rigged," he muttered as he dug through a bin of tools he'd brought with him. He stood back up, holding a hammer and a screwdriver. "You need better security around here," he continued to grumble, and shot her a concerned look.

"Listen, sweetheart," he called through the door, his tone much improved for Gina's sake. "You're going to hear some loud thuds, but don't you worry. I'll have you out of there in no time."

"It's real dark...and my shirt's going out," a tiny voice said.

"Oh? Well, don't worry," Greg assured her, his forehead wrinkled in confusion. "I'll get you out before that happens. Can't have your shirt going out." He sounded so completely bewildered that Angelica almost laughed in spite of the tense situation.

Greg attacked the exposed hinges with the hammer and screwdriver, knocking out the pin that held the halves together. He repeated the operation on the other two hinges, then pulled the door out of the door frame. A small compact body hit his as soon as he set the heavy door against the wall.

"Thank you. Oh, thank you, Mr. Greg. You saved me!"

Greg lifted the girl into his arms, smiled that heart-stopping smile of his, and wiped away Gina's tears with his thumb. "And thank you very much for the very nice thank-you. Tell me, Gina, what were you doing in there?"

"'Member I said my shirt was going out? My mom said it glows in the dark...but I never get to wear it in the dark on account of that I have to go to bed just when it's *getting* dark and it's a...daytime to wear thing. So I went in the closet to see it light up, but the lock locked me in."

"Wow. That's some story. You've got to promise me not to go in any more closets till I can check out all the locks. I'd worry myself into an ulcer if I thought you'd do this when I wasn't here to get you out. Okay, sweetheart? Promise?"

Gina nodded with enthusiasm and wrapped her plump arms around Greg's neck. "I promise."

"Great," Greg said, and hugged the little girl back. "Now, where's your mother?"

"She was cleaning the bathrooms, and I said I'd go back to the Kids' Corner and play. But the closet was on my way, and I wanted to see my shirt light up." Gina frowned. "Am I in trouble?"

"Not with me. Let's go on up to the Kids' Corner. Angelica, would you stay here and watch that no one knocks the door over?"

Angelica watched as Greg carried Gina down the hall toward Kids' Corner, bouncing her on his hip. The child's breathing had evened out, her upset forgotten in the reassuring arms of a gentle giant. Angelica breathed a sigh. One more problem solved. She wondered how many more the day would bring.

At least she knew Gina would stay out of trouble at the Kids' Corner, a day-care-cum-baby-sitting service for children of all ages. The older ones played with the younger ones, helping the adults who volunteered there while seeking the jobs that would get their lives back on track.

Gina kissed Greg and squealed with glee as they turned the corner into the hallway where the day care center was located. With the little girl, he acted as if nothing was wrong, but Angelica had seen something in Greg's eyes. Some sort of worry that had compelled him to take Gina where she'd gone by herself countless other times.

"You're so good with children," Angelica said, when Greg returned. "Have you been around them much?"

"No. I just figure they're little people and I treat them that way. And I try to remember what it was like for me at that age. Like being ordered to do something that made no sense when you didn't want to. Or doing something that seems like a good idea and winding up hurt, then getting yelled at for it when you felt bad enough all on your own."

"Speaking of being told and not told reasons, would you mind telling me why she couldn't just walk down the hall to the Kids' Corner?"

"Because maybe it isn't as safe inside the mission

as I'll bet it once was. I think we need to post
guards—some of the regular residents that you know
and trust—and restrict access to the residential areas
of the building.''

"Guards? Why?''

"Because this lock didn't get stuck any more than
that fire last night was an accident. Someone tossed
a flare into that Dumpster and—Angelica, that lock,''
he said pointing to the knob on the closet door, "is
a double-keyed lock set. Someone locked the door
and broke the key off in the lock on the inside. Even
if it had been someone with a key who got locked in
there, it wouldn't have done any good.'' He reached
in and twisted the bulb, illuminating the interior of
the closet. "The lightbulb wasn't burned out, either.
This was no accident.''

Angelica felt suddenly cold, and went immediately
to the hook inside the doorway of the closet. The key
usually hanging there was missing. Her hand shook
as she rested it over her heart. They had endangered
a child.

"Okay. I'll post guards,'' she conceded. "But
who—and where?''

Greg answered before Angelica realized she'd
asked the question aloud. "There aren't that many
spots where they'd need to be posted. Any adult not
working can take a turn. It's no different from cleaning bathrooms or scrubbing floors to earn their keep.''

"I suppose not. Will you take care of it? I want to
go check on the children. I don't suppose they should
have the run of the place anymore, either. Maybe I
should call a meeting.'' She turned to walk away, but
stopped. She looked up at Greg, tears swimming in

her eyes. "It was supposed to be a place where people could come in from the street and feel safe. It was supposed to feel like a home. Like one big happy family. Now it's starting to feel like an armed camp."

She turned and walked away. After checking on the Kids' Corner, she had an appointment with the head of a large corporation that was in search of a charity to use as a tax deduction. She intended to convince her father's old friend to put North Riverside Mission at the top of his list for consideration. The Judges weren't going to stop her. They weren't!

Chapter Four

Angelica entered the dining hall, calling out a general "Good Morning" to the few residents having their first meal of the day. They were the lucky ones who had to be up and out to the jobs that were the ticket to their new lives. Seeing them smiling and eager to be off gladdened her heart. She really was making a difference.

Then she noticed Greg sitting near the doors to the kitchen. Hunched over his coffee, he seemed to be in a world all his own. Even from where she stood, his blue eyes looked haunted, his body language shouted misery.

A week had gone by since he'd intervened in the confrontation with Mr. Jackson. And in those seven days she'd tried to tuck away the feelings she'd discovered for him. But they just wouldn't stay buried.

Rosa, Emanuel's niece, put her arms up, begging for attention. Emanuel took care of Rosa most mornings and Angelica always tried to lend a hand with the baby during the active breakfast period. Angelica lifted Rosa onto her hip. Remembering Greg's love of children she decided a baby's happy grin would go a long way toward cheering him up. It was a perfect solution that would let Angelica help him without having to give too much of herself.

"Mornin'," he mumbled, when she reached the table. At first he didn't even glance up, but with Rosa vying for his attention Greg finally lifted his head. His gaze locked with hers for a long heartbeat, then slid away toward Rosa. Then his bright, blue eyes sparkled in the morning light as Rosa squealed her own joyous greeting at him. The baby dove into Greg's arms, and he accepted her weight as well as her baby adoration.

"How's my little sweetheart this morning?" Greg said, hugging the baby against his broad chest.

"Ab ab baa baaa," answered Rosa, her face wreathed in happiness.

"Well I'm so glad to hear that!"

Helpless against the quick flash of boyish charm that showed through his rough facade as he tickled the toddler on her plump tummy, Angelica smiled. He'd changed a little more each day since his arrival, and the change was more than just wearing clean clothes and taking daily showers. He seemed to be more at peace with himself, which was a big step toward his reentry into the world. And that was why his troubled expression this morning so dismayed her.

It was a foolish reaction to what was probably a perfectly normal mood swing, she knew, but seeing him look so downhearted reminded her that he was by no means healed of whatever trauma had put him on the streets. As she often did, Angelica wished she could ask Greg about his past. Then she'd pull back from the impulse. She knew she couldn't risk getting any closer to him. She could barely handle her attraction to him now. Her goal was only to help him and he *was* closer to being able to get on with his life, she told herself. Closer to being a productive member of society. Closer to leaving North Riverside Mission. And her.

Angelica's heart stuttered in her chest. That was what she wanted for him, wasn't it?

Confused by her ping-pong thoughts, and desperate to strike up an innocuous conversation that wouldn't involve examining her feelings for him, Angelica cast about for a safe subject. That was when she noticed the meager breakfast in front of him.

"Is that all you're having to eat?"

"Lead coffee and charred toast. Breakfast of champions." He tickled the baby's tummy and offered her a blackened toast point. Greg flashed Angelica a smile, but the smile didn't reflect in his troubled eyes.

"Breakfast for the dull-witted, you mean?" She grabbed the toast away from the baby. "You can't give that to Rosa. All that charcoal will upset her stomach," Angelica teased.

Rosa squealed as if she, too, got the joke, and Greg chuckled at the baby's glee if not at Angelica's attempt at humor. "This is all I have time for," he said. "Besides, Manny was experimenting with hash and ketchup when I went in to grab a quick cup of coffee."

She tsked. "Why do you tease him so incessantly?"

He winked at her and passed Rosa across the table. "It's a guy thing, Miss DeVoe. Besides, he deserves every second of it."

Angelica laughed. "Sometimes he's a little over the top, I'll admit. But he gets great deals on fish and if it's fried and served with ketchup, it's—"

"Don't even go there," Greg groaned. "It's too early to even think about fried fish and ketchup."

"Speaking of early, where are you off to in such a hurry on your day off?" Angelica asked, curious in spite of all her stern promises to treat him just like any other resident.

"I promised to help Josey Harding move her family into their new house today."

"Oh, Greg, you shouldn't be moving furniture."

Greg shook his head in disgust. "It's been a week. I have to get started on some of the bigger projects around here that you've been putting off for me. I'm almost like new. Just three more days, and Dr. Satie said she'd take out the stitches. It was no big deal."

"Hmm...let's see. There was lots of blood. An undisclosed number of stitches. I even seem to remember you nearly passing out." Angelica pursed her lips. "It certainly seemed serious enough at the time."

He grinned ruefully and took a bite of his charred toast. As he chewed, his eyes grew more serious and dropped back to his nearly empty plate. "To put your mind at rest, I'm only doing the driving. Josey can't handle a truck, so I volunteered. Otherwise, she'd have had to wait till Saturday for her brother. And those kids're too excited about their new place to wait till then."

Angelica smiled in spite of a suddenly heavy heart.

"The neighborhood's losing a great family. I tried to get Homes for Restoration to work on some of the abandoned houses up here, but the banks won't issue mortgages in North Riverside. The neighborhood's been red-lined."

Greg frowned. "That's illegal."

Angelica let out a tired sigh and laid her cheek against Rosa's fuzzy head, where it lay on her shoulder. Sometimes she felt as if she were perpetually swimming upstream. "Oh, they've got all kinds of bureaucratic excuses, but the fact is they don't want to lend money on homes that might be worth next to nothing in a few years. That's why Josey's new house isn't here."

Greg said nothing for several long seconds. He just stared at her with slightly narrowed eyes. "It isn't your fault. There's only so much any of us can do to change the world, Angelica. Don't beat yourself up. You're doing a great job here. Maybe I could talk to some of the organizers today and see if there's a way around the banks. Maybe we can come up with a couple of ideas." He looked at his watch. "I'd better get a move on."

Angelica watched as Greg gulped down the rest of his coffee and hurried off. She stared after him, wondering why he'd really volunteered to drive Josey's truck. There had been something in his eyes, the way they'd slid back to his toast when he talked about his reason for driving the truck today.

Pretty and blond, Josey had been widowed for three years. Was Greg attracted to her? They certainly had a lot in common. Down on her luck and homeless just like Greg, Josey Harding had four children ranging in age from ten to five. Was there more to his offer than kindness?

Angelica wasn't sure of anything except that the possibility that he liked Josey bothered her too much. She *had* to get a handle on her feelings for him. She stood, with Rosa nodding off on her shoulder, and wandered to the window just in time to see Greg, Josey, her children and a few of the men from the mission walking toward the bus stop. Greg ruffled five-year-old Tate's blond hair and hoisted him onto his shoulders. Greg was so different from any man she'd ever met. Maybe that was why she had these feelings for him. He was certainly a different kind of man from her father...

"I know why you're doing this," Gaither DeVoe had shouted. "It's spite. You know how embarrassed I'll be, and how worried your mother will be to have you living in that pit you call a neighborhood mission. It's a homeless shelter full of alcoholics and drug addicts. You just love that, don't you? Sometimes I think you'd marry the first hobo who asked, if you thought it would hurt and embarrass us."

"Living at the mission isn't about rebellion," Angelica said. "And it isn't a homeless shelter. It's supposed to help the residents get on their feet. This isn't about you and mother. It's about doing with my life what the Lord would have me do. It's about being where He wants me to be. It's about serving Him."

"Ever since you found this new religion of yours, God is your excuse to do exactly as you want, and cast aside your duty to this family. If I say black, you say white. You do the exact opposite of what we

want—and have for years! That's what this is really all about!''

She tried to push the memory of the ugly scene out of her mind. He'd been wrong about her reasons for working with the people of the North side, but could he be right about the rest? Was rebellion what her attraction to Greg was all about? Everything in her spurned the thought. They didn't understand her—had never understood her. What did the opinions of her parents matter anyway? They had given up the right to comment on her life when they'd stolen from her and from her dreams. And all this speculation was ridiculous, anyway. Greg was nothing to her but the new handyman—someone she was trying to rehabilitate. That was all!

And pigs fly, a traitorous voice whispered in her heart.

Greg walked out of the truck rental office and sauntered to the curb. He saw a classic Ford Mustang parked about three hundred feet farther down the street. Sticking out his thumb, he watched his lifelong buddy, Internal Affairs Detective Jim Lovell, pull out into traffic. They'd grown up across the street from each other. Greg trusted Jim completely, and he'd asked for his help.

When the car stopped next to him, Greg jumped in. "Is it all set up?"

"All set."

Greg slumped down in the seat, dropped his head back and shut his eyes. "Man, this is a mess."

"I thought this case was supposed to be a breeze—practically a vacation."

"That's what it was billed as, but I had a funny feeling going in. Within minutes inside, I knew it wasn't going to be a cakewalk."

"The commissioner's not going to be a happy camper about this. He won't like his cousin being accused."

"Tough. Either the man's on the take or he's as incompetent as they come," Greg said bitterly. "Most or all of the men under him are." When he twisted to look over at Jim, the stitches in his side pulled, reminding him of just how sure he was that at least two officers from the Third deserved to be taken down. He'd finally put some clues together. "If Worth and Gates had Jackson in custody before as Angelica says, they knew who the more likely candidate was to cause a squad car to be called. They tried to get me hurt. I just haven't figured out why."

Lovell looked thoughtful. "Maybe so you wouldn't be able to protect Ms. DeVoe. Whatever's going on though, we'll get to the bottom of this, Greg, I promise. But in the meantime, you're sticking your neck out a mile on this one."

Greg squeezed the bridge of his nose. "Someone has to."

"How's your side doing?"

Greg let out a disgusted snort. "A pain in more ways than one. Every time I move, the stitches yank."

"How many?"

"I didn't ask. She didn't tell." Greg glanced up at the Tower, the multistoried police headquarters building, and took a deep breath. This was it.

Lovell glanced over at Greg, his brown eyes solemn. "You realize that calling us in isn't going to

make you too popular around here once the word gets
out?''

Greg shrugged and pushed himself farther up in his
seat, as Jim pulled inside the garage under the headquarters building. "Being a cop isn't a popularity
contest. Like I said, someone has to do what's right.
I have no choice. You know that."

"Yeah. But right isn't always the easiest or the
safest route to take. I'm proud of you, buddy. You're
a good cop."

"I'm a tired cop." Greg sighed and opened the
door. Over the gleaming roof of the car that he,
Tommy and Jim had worked to restore back in their
teens, he added, "Beat. Sick of not really making a
difference. After this is over, I'm going to take a leave
of absence. I have to find out who I am. I feel like I
lost myself somewhere."

Jim walked around the hood of the car and led the
way into the building. He waited until they reached
the privacy of the stairwell. "You shouldn't have
jumped back in so soon."

"Thinking about Jessie was driving me crazy. The
captain thought another case would help."

"A few sessions with the department shrink would
have helped more. It helped me. Here we are," he
said as he pulled open the heavy door and walked
across the hall to a conference room.

There were three men already in the room: Harry
Donovan, Riverside's police commissioner, Captain
Glen Harris, Greg's boss on the narcotics squad, and
Jim Lovell's boss, Captain Joe Torres, head of Inter-
nal Affairs. All three men were in their mid- to late-
fifties, ran toward paunchy, and had hair threaded

with gray. There the similarity ended. Donovan was the most political and visible commissioner the city had ever seen. Some thought he had an eye on the mayor's job. Torres backed his men one-hundred-and-ten percent, which was good since they were the most hated group in the department: cops who investigated other cops. And his own boss—tough and cantankerous, but he loved his men and had cried harder at Jessie's funeral than her own father. Greg and all the guys on the squad would walk through fire for the man, and he for them.

After introductions were completed, the commissioner asked what the meeting was about. Greg explained, "I was sent to infiltrate the North Riverside Christian Mission. An informant fingered the woman who runs it as the kingpin for trafficking in the neighborhood. But there's no evidence to support the claim. In fact, from what I can find out, the problem is a local gang called the Judges and—" Greg glanced at Lovell, who nodded in encouragement.

"Well, spit it out," the IAD captain urged.

Greg fisted his hand under the conference table. He was about to open up an even bigger can of worms than the one he walked in on at Angelica's mission. He glanced at his own captain, then Jim Lovell. "There's something not quite right going on at the Third, sir."

"Excuse me!" Donovan snapped. "What the— Are you saying what I think you are? You mean to tell me I was called here to listen to some long-haired, bearded freak of a cop casting aspersions on the good name of Jerry Rossi?"

Torres, the IAD captain, stepped in to the fray

while his own boss shot daggers at the commissioner. "Here's what Peterson's got so far," he said as he passed around copies of the photos Greg had taken and his report on the incident with Sam Jackson. "I've checked him out, Commissioner, and I assure you he isn't an officer to make such an accusation lightly. He's been decorated three times for valor since he came on the force. And he nearly lost his life two months ago in the line of duty. His contribution to the squad has been invaluable. Isn't that right, Harris?"

"Greg's the best undercover officer I've got. I'll admit, I was as shocked as you when I heard this stuff, but if Greg says something's rotten at the Third, then I guess it needs checking out."

"Do all your men dress like this?" the commissioner sneered.

Did the guy think he *liked* looking like this? Greg wondered. He shot a glance toward Jim Lovell, who had to cover his mouth to hide a grin. "I'm undercover, sir," Greg said in response before Captain Harris's legendary temper erupted in his defense. "I can't be expected to blend in on the streets and do my job if I have to show up for meetings in regulation uniform, clean-shaven and with my hair in a regulation cut in order to get the same respect some spit-and-polish uniform would."

Donovan frowned, his face now deepened to a dull red. "No, I don't suppose you do. I apologize, Detective. I rarely meet our undercover officers while they're working in the field."

Ten minutes later, Greg was running low on patience again. He'd gone over his last week in detail.

He couldn't believe anyone could still believe Angelica was involved—but the commissioner did. He seemed determined that if his cousin was going to look bad, so was some civilian out there. And Angelica was the fall guy. "Why are you so sure this Angelica DeVoe isn't involved?" the commissioner asked again.

Greg sighed. This was like trying to convince a bull not to charge. "It isn't her," he said once again. "I searched. I turned that place upside down. There's nothing there to find! She's just what she seems to be. She's trying to help those people."

"Look, son, no spoiled, rich broad leaves behind the kind of life she did to live in poverty in North Riverside."

"Don't call her a broad. It's disrespectful." Greg knew he'd made a mistake the second the words left his mouth. This is why Donovan had kept pushing! He'd wanted to trip Greg up. And he had.

The commissioner raised a speculative eyebrow. "Are you getting personally involved with this woman, Detective?"

"She's not involved with drugs *or* me," Greg said through gritted teeth.

The commissioner tossed a file across the conference table toward Greg. "She was a wild kid. Even got picked up a couple of times. A leopard doesn't change its spots."

"Begging your pardon, sir," Greg countered, more calmly this time. "But the Lord can move mountains—and He can change lives." Greg glanced at the file. "And this is a juvenile file. It's supposed to be sealed."

"Nothing in this department is sealed if I want to look at it, Detective. And what are you—some throwback to the sixties' hippy-Jesus-freak days?"

Watching Glen Harris trying to rein in his temper and still try to correct a superior officer was a sight to behold. He growled, "What Greg Peterson is, sir, is an exemplary officer and on that merit alone he has a right to his opinion *and* to have it given a fair hearing. His instincts about people are as good as his record. If Detective Peterson says this woman's clean, and if he claims her religion changed her, then we should assume he's correct. Because so far he has been."

Captain Joe Torres, IAD, tossed a different file on the local Precinct toward the commissioner. "I think if you'll take a good look at this, you'll see the real problem, sir. There's a pattern there that can't be denied. Either that station is nearly seventy-five-percent dirty, or nearly everyone on the roster is just plain stupid. Captain Rossi included! Not only is their conviction rate downright ridiculous, but, as Peterson said, and as we've been able to corroborate in the last two days, they patrol the same time every day. The pushers go inside, the car drives by, the pushers waltz back out and get down to business as usual. And you have his report on the Jackson incident and Peterson's encounter with Worth and Gates. This is something IAD should look into, sir. I think we should pull Peterson and launch a full-scale investigation."

Greg no longer agreed, even though he'd be off the hook and not have to continue to lie to Angelica. Something in him rebelled at leaving the mission—leaving her—unprotected. He still didn't have enough proof that Teddy Leach was right, and you didn't besmirch the name of fellow officers without solid proof. He shot a glance at his captain, who took the cue as if they'd rehearsed it. "Commissioner, if on-the-street sale of drugs is involved then that part of the investigation is the Narcotics Squad's territory. Of course, if dirty cops are involved, then IAD needs to be involved. I propose we coordinate efforts. Keep Peterson in place, blitz the neighborhood with other undercover men buying. Set up something in the way of a sting to catch as many of these guys as possible."

Commissioner Harry Donovan screwed up his face in concentration. "It's certainly looking bad for those boys at the Third. I've known Jerry Rossi all my life, and though I can't bring myself to believe this of him, I can't ignore what Peterson has seen. The photographs and that gash in his side are proof that there's a problem. Torres and Harris, you coordinate your units and clean up this mess. Until it's over, though, I don't want to hear a thing."

Greg breathed a nearly audible sigh of relief. "I'm sure Ms. DeVoe will cooperate by letting me set up a base of operations at the mission," he told the four other men.

"I'm still not convinced the woman isn't involved," Donovan said. "I don't want you to tell her anything, either. Keep up the front you've established, and make sure she's not involved."

Greg couldn't believe his ears. "Sir, I have made sure. I'm trying to do the best job I can. And I can't concentrate on the drug problem if I'm forced to follow dead leads. Everything that informant gave us on her was lies. She's clean. She's trying to help rebuild

the North side, but she's in someone's way. I think
it's the Third Precinct and the Judges.''

The commissioner's gaze rose from the report on
the Jackson incident. ''They were really going to skip
Mirandizing Jackson because they decided he was too
drunk to understand them? Unbelievable!''

''Yes, sir, it was. Ms. DeVoe charged up to them
and told them how to handle the arrest, or we
wouldn't have a case right now. The last time he was
brought in for abusing his wife and kids, his lawyer
had him out from under in days because of the sloppy
procedures at the Third.''

Donovan shook his head. ''My decision stands.
You tell her nothing. If you can't handle it, we'll put
someone else in there. If she's as innocent as you say,
then she has nothing to fear.''

Chapter Five

If she's as innocent as you say, she has nothing to fear. The commissioner's infuriating words reverberated in his mind like the rumble of a swollen river about to crest. How dare Harry Donovan decide that she was guilty until proven innocent? His head pounding with the granddaddy of all tension headaches, Greg searched for answers. By giving the outcome to the Lord, he was usually able to reach some measure of peace in situations that fell outside the realm of his control, but this time his emotions roiled inside him, washing away all his defenses.

The bus driver called out the name of the stop before his, and Greg gritted his teeth, praying for the strength to step back into the lies. He was not so far gone down the wrong path that the irony of his request escaped him. He stepped off the bus at the corner of Rockland and Center, and looked around at the litter and refuse that had come to define North Riverside.

She has nothing to fear.

Angelica lived day in and day out in this swamp of debris and decline, all the while trying to change the unchangeable. Trying to stem the flow of misery and pain. And what was her reward? To be suspected of wrongdoing. To have a Judas planted in her home. Greg fisted his hands.

She has nothing to fear.

Greg remembered the other threat Angelica lived under. How dare Donovan assume there was a way that she could be safe when she'd made enemies in a street gang? Donovan—who lived on the South side in a sixteen-room residence that sat atop the bluff overlooking the reservoir. Donovan—who didn't have bars on his windows or triple locks on his bedroom door. Donovan—who didn't have to worry about a gang's threats of revenge.

Greg forced his thoughts back to the task ahead of him—a role he'd quickly come to loathe. But his hands were tied. It was wrong. He felt it deep within his soul. There'd been no talking to the high and mighty commissioner. He'd stubbornly refused to budge. Angelica was still a suspect—however unlikely—and Greg was under orders not to take her into his confidence. In fact, his superiors even wanted him to bug the mission, her office, and, worst of all, her apartment. He detested the very idea of invading her privacy again. Searching her apartment before he'd really gotten to know her had been bad enough.

And he still had to go on with the drug buys. Which put her funding in jeopardy if he got caught. So here he was, returning to a place she'd started to give solace and hope to troubled people, and putting it all at risk.

Judas, his conscience screamed at him. *This isn't right!*

How had he gotten so far on the other side of the fence from one of his superiors—so far from the goal he'd set at his brother's grave? For years he'd used anyone and anything if it meant putting one more pusher behind bars—taking one more kilo of drugs off the street. And worse, why, when he was in such a state of confusion about where his life was headed, did he feel that turning around and going back would bring him closer to knowing who he was?

Greg stopped and looked up at the late evening sky. *What do I do, Lord? What do I do?*

But as had happened more and more, the deeper undercover he'd gone, the voice that answered asked only questions: *Who are you, Greg Peterson? Where have you gone? Where are you going?* Greg shook his head and shifted his backpack to the other shoulder. He didn't know. He didn't even know where to look for himself. He only knew that he had begun to believe that the answers lay somewhere other than in his job.

And he knew one more thing.

He knew that he didn't want to lie to Angelica anymore. Just that morning he'd thought it would be his last meal with her, his last lie before she learned of his duplicity. He'd thought it was his last chance to see her smile. And because he dreaded the loss of her in his life, however on the fringe he'd kept her, Greg had had trouble gathering the courage to even look at her when she'd approached him. He'd even given serious consideration to ignoring her in the hope that she'd go away.

But she'd used a secret weapon. Angelica and Rosa's combined lilac and baby powder scents had enveloped him, and he'd been utterly defeated. He'd looked up and lost his heart to an impossible vision. Angelica, smiling down at him with a baby on her hip, had looked so—so *right!* And that rightness had made him wish for more in his life than duty and obsession.

They'd looked so right that he'd let himself sink into the dream for just a split second. It had been the first time in nine years that he'd allowed himself a thought of a future that didn't include guns, drugs—and lying. It had been a split second too long to allow himself to dream, because he'd instinctively reached out and taken Rosa into his arms—as if he had a right to touch such innocence when he had blood on his hands.

And then he'd grasped onto the familiarity of Angelica's growing concern for his rotten eating habits like a man going down for the third time.

Because that's what he had been.

Now he was in even further over his head. But he was no longer drowning in the river of life. He was being buried under the muck of his own deceit. And he felt even dirtier thinking of the high-tech listening devices that rattled around in his backpack. They were the biggest lie of all.

"There are no second chances with me," Angelica had told him. Her warning haunted him as much as did his own conscience, because, however out of

character it seemed for her to be so unforgiving, he knew that she had meant every word.

Even Jim Lovell hadn't understood Greg's dread. He'd told Greg to look at the extension of his assignment as a way to stay on at the mission and prove her innocence. As a way to be there to keep Angelica safe from whoever was threatening her. But then Jim hadn't seen the vision Greg had that morning. Jim didn't understand that nothing was as critical as the lies. That the longer they remained to fester below the surface of his relationship with Angelica, the more damage they would do.

That the vision of Angelica and a baby all their own was lost before it ever had a chance of coming true.

Lost in thought, Greg didn't notice the unusually large crowd gathered on the front steps of the mission until the chatter reached his ears and yanked him out of his reverie. *Let your attention wander at any time while undercover and you'll die.* Glen Harris had given him those words to live by during his undercover training. He'd never before forgotten.

Glancing around, he took in the crowd and saw nothing suspicious. People in neighboring houses sat on their fronts steps chatting. Nothing unusual there. But three gang members stood about a hundred yards down the street. They seemed to be waiting for something to happen, but looked poised to scatter. The muscles at the back of Greg's neck tightened.

Something wasn't right.

Greg scanned the crowd for Angelica, and found her sitting in front of the mission with several children gathered around. The pink late-afternoon sun brought out the red highlights in her hair even more than usual, and her creamy skin nearly begged to be caressed. She and Rosa, sleeping on her lap, looked like a dream come true.

Giving him a little smile as he walked up the steps toward her, she said, "You look as if you had a pretty tiring day."

"Yeah, but it's a good kind of tired. Josey and the kids are unpacking boxes even as we speak." Greg looked around, unable to shake the feeling of impending doom. "What's everybody doing out here?"

"There's an odor in the building. I can't figure out where it's coming from. It kept getting worse, so we opened the windows and came outside. Manny called the gas company just in case it's a leak. They still haven't arrived. Most of the repairmen don't like to come up to the North side anymore."

Angelica could see anger leap into Greg's eyes. "It's okay, Greg. Those men are just worried about their own safety. They have families who depend on them. They watch the evening news and listen to the radio all day in their trucks. They see and hear only the bad about this neighborhood. It's understandable."

"I'll take a look," he growled. "My father's a plumber. I learned to run gas pipe when I was fourteen."

"It doesn't smell like gas to me. Why don't you just relax for a little while like the rest of us?" She patted the step next to her and smiled, hoping he'd sit still for a while. He was forever running off somewhere on some self-appointed mission of repair. If they never got a chance to talk, how was she supposed to help the man? "We've been having a great time enjoying the evening air, haven't we, kids?"

Even though all the children smiled up at him and invited him to stay, Greg shook his head. "I really ought to check it out."

"Then I'll come with you," she offered.

But Greg shook his head again. "Too dangerous. In fact, you all ought to move farther away from the building. Just in case. Why not go on back to the Tot Lot?"

"If we shouldn't be on the steps, then you certainly shouldn't go inside."

Greg flashed a sardonic smile. "I know. Ms. DeVoe wants no heroics from her employees."

"Please, don't throw my words back at me. I thought we got past that. Was I wrong?"

"No. And I understand that you don't want anyone to get hurt." He backed away toward the open front doors. Angelica saw the same stubborn look in his eyes that she'd seen when he'd confronted her about how he would handle any intruders that he might encounter in the night.

"Be careful," she warned.

"I know what I'm doing, and with the windows open it's not all that dangerous even if it is a gas leak. Besides, you're probably right that it's nothing serious. I won't be long. But move back, just in case," he added before disappearing inside.

Silently admitting defeat, Angelica directed the others to the Tot Lot. She imagined that she looked a bit like the Pied Piper as she led the group down the steps, around the corner on the wide sidewalk, and into the playground through the gate on the side street.

An hour later, when the pink light of dusk had just given way to the darkness of night, Angelica spotted Greg striding across the basketball courts and asphalt playground toward the fenced-in Tot Lot. "All clear," he told her. "The gas company showed up about half an hour ago and set up some fans to clear the place out."

"So it really was a gas leak?"

Greg glanced away, then back at her. "Yeah, it was gas. It's—fixed now. Who blew out all the pilot lights? Manny?"

"No. One of the neighborhood boys had stopped by to see his girlfriend. He smelled it too, and told us to get out. He said he'd turn off the gas at the main and blow out the pilots just in case."

"He averted a real problem. Who did you say he was?"

"Adam Jones. He lives two streets over. He's a good boy. He's the father of Jean Ann's baby. He wants to marry her, but at fifteen and seventeen they're both too young. And thank God, they know it."

"Fifteen?" Greg asked with a grimace.

Angelica nodded. "Jean Ann's parents were abusive already, which is how I wound up involved. She ran away when she found out about the baby, and Adam brought her here."

Greg shook his head. "What people do to their kids."

"That's what I finally got across to Adam and Jean Ann. They've decided on adoption, and marriage later—when they're ready. They want what's best for their baby. She wants to go to college. And Adam's a straight-*A* student." Angelica frowned. "You know, it was strange—Adam was furious when he left here. And he said the oddest thing. He told me to take good care of them, as if he didn't expect to be back. I asked Jean Ann, but she said they hadn't argued."

Greg seemed to stiffen. "I'd like to talk to him," he said, frowning now, too. "Do you know where he lives? Exactly?"

"No, but I'm sure Jean Ann does." Angelica pointed toward a young, obviously pregnant teen.

"I'll be back in a while. Everybody can go back inside now," he told the group, then walked toward Jean Ann.

"Greg!" Angelica called. He stopped and turned back to her. "Did you fix the leak, or do I owe the gas company?"

He hesitated. "There wasn't a leak...exactly. I'll tell you about it later. Lock up till I get back." He turned and was gone, swallowed up by the approaching darkness and the crowd of people headed back toward the mission.

"Now, what did he mean by that? It was either a leak or it wasn't," she said to herself, and sank down onto a swing, watching the lights come on inside the mission and along the surrounding streets. Night had fallen. It was time to go inside where she was supposed to feel safe. She shivered. She wouldn't feel safe until Greg returned. Angelica wondered why that was.

And she wondered if she would ever feel safe again after Greg Peters moved on with his life.

* * *

Greg walked the two blocks to Albert Street and headed up toward 346, where Jean Ann told him Adam Jones lived. She'd also told him that Adam was constantly harassed by the Judges for not joining the gang. Asking Angelica to take care of his girl and their baby sounded too final to Greg. Way too final.

When he added in the open propane canister that he'd found spewing gas in the basement, Greg figured Adam must have suspected the person or persons responsible. If he had then decided to confront that person, the boy could be in trouble.

Greg owed him. Because he didn't want to think what would have happened if he hadn't turned off those pilots.

How the Judges had arranged this latest "accident," Greg intended to figure out. Later. Right now, he hoped to head off a confrontation that might see an end to Adam Jones. A crash echoed from the alley between the first and second set of row homes that made up the three-hundred block of Albert Street. Greg drew his revolver from the holster at the small of his back, and entered the dark alley.

Just as his eyes adjusted to the light, his foot connected with something solid. Greg looked down. Adam Jones lay on his back, eyes closed, arms and legs limp. Was he too late? Again? Jessie Cushing's pale face swam in front of Greg's eyes before a moan pulled him back to the present.

Dropping to his knees among the trash and the weeds that grew in the cracks of the cement, he felt Adam latch on to his sleeve. "Adam? Are you Adam?" Greg asked.

The boy nodded as he gasped for breath.

Greg grabbed the tiny cell phone he kept with him at all times. When the 911 dispatcher came on the line, Greg told her his badge number to cut through red tape, then his location, and his need for an ambulance. Adam had been shot. Greg pulled out a clean handkerchief and pressed on a wound on the boy's forehead. "I've called for an ambulance," he told the boy as he applied pressure to the wound. "You hang in there."

"Go. Propane. Blow the place…up. Jud—" The word cut off while still in the boy's throat. He stiffened and gasped, his pain clearly excruciating.

"Save your strength. It's okay. I'll be right back. I'll get your parents."

"They're…out. Y-you work…there. Is she…all right?"

"Jean Ann? Yeah. Calm down. I found the tank and turned it off."

"Yeah. Good. Tell me… Is the angel right? About after?"

"Angelica DeVoe?" At the boy's weak nod, Greg figured he wasn't the only one who thought of Angelica as an angel. "Was she right about what?" he asked.

"Is it never—too late?" Adam gasped out. "Did He die…for us? Is just believing…enough?"

Greg looked back at the street. Where was the ambulance? Procedures ran through his head. Call for a unit and an ambulance. Until it arrived, question the victim. Maybe nail down the name of the perp. Then Greg looked back at Adam's frightened face. He suddenly didn't care about procedures. He lifted the boy to cradle him in his arms. "Yeah, it's all true. You just have to believe that He came to save you. Just you. He loved you that much. Just ask Him into your heart and He'll do the rest."

"I want to. The angel. She told me. But...me and Jean Ann...the baby."

"Remember the good thief? He wasn't good in his life. He wasn't falsely convicted like Jesus. He was crucified because he was a criminal. He mocked Jesus right along with the other thief. He's the good thief because in the end he repented and believed who Jesus was."

Adam stiffened and gasped, agony written on features too young to know such pain. Such fear. But somehow Adam managed to speak again. "Whole life...spent in this awful place. Don't...want that...forever."

"Just believe. Just ask," Greg promised. "But don't give up. There's lots for you to do right here on earth. Fight for Jean Ann. For your parents. Fight to live."

Adam closed his eyes and nodded.

"I'm going to call this in again, Adam. You need help now."

Adam grabbed Greg's shirt with surprising strength. "Watch out...Judge w—" The boy's breath hitched in his throat, then his hand went slack as his eyes rolled back in his head.

Anxious, Greg felt for a pulse. It was weak, but it was there. "Fight, Adam. Fight to stay with us," he urged.

Greg knelt, holding the boy, not wanting to lay him back in the trash-filled alley. Then, suddenly, the horror of Jessie's death began to replay itself, taking him from one nightmare into another....

The blood soaking his shirt was his own now, and gunfire burst around him. It was a young woman, too young to die, who lay in his arms. He felt the emptiness again. The guilt again. It crushed in on him. The futility. The loss.

The sound of a car door closing out on the street brought Greg back to the present. Back to a different tragedy. He laid Adam Jones down, and picked up his gun. Tucking it back in the holster, he made sure that it was hidden under his loose shirt. He saw a middle-aged couple get out of their car, and forced himself to stand. To leave Adam behind.

"What do you want?" the woman asked when she saw Greg emerge from the darkness. She stared at the blood on his shirt and hands, and drew back against the man. The man stepped in front of the woman.

"There's a kid in the alley. He was shot," Greg said. "Could you go to 346 and see if his parents are home? I already called for an ambulance."

"Did you say 346?"

The alarm in the man's voice worried Greg. "346. It's Adam Jones. I went after him because it sounded as if he'd gone looking for trouble when he left the mission."

"No!" the woman cried. "Not Adam! Please, dear God. Not my Adam."

Greg swallowed. "Mr. and Mrs. Jones?" he asked, and wondered if Adam's decision for Christ would console these people at all. But as he watched Adam's parents run toward the alley, and as the sound of sirens began to fill the air, he knew they were about to enter a place where there were no words adequate to comfort and console. He knew. He'd watched his own parents suffer while they waited to hear if Tommy would live or die.

Please, God. Don't let his parents suffer the same way mine did.

Chapter Six

❧

Angelica stared out her window at the litter-strewn street below. The early morning breeze wafted in, stirring the lace curtains so they skimmed across her arms. She glanced at the display on her clock. Three-thirty.

Hours had come and gone since Greg left in search of Adam Jones. Hours since sirens had split the night and added to the cacophony of loud television sets, music blaring from passing cars and an out-of-control family squabble across the street. She sighed, not understanding her own agitation. It was a typical North Riverside night.

But this night felt different.

Tonight, there had been another "accident" at the mission. An "accident" she had a feeling Greg would say had not been an accident at all. Tonight, Greg Peters was out there and had been for hours. Though he hadn't said so, she suspected that he was searching for Adam, who might have gone looking for trouble.

And so tonight, she'd spent hours in prayer for their safety. But she couldn't shake the worry she felt that they had both found more trouble than they could handle.

Some minutes later, a car turned the corner and came to a stop in front of the building. Moonlight glinted off Greg's golden hair as he stepped out of the dark interior. He bent down to say something to the driver before turning away to vault up the front steps.

Angelica turned from the window when she lost sight of him behind the thick foliage of the oak tree that stood sentinel next to the high front steps of the building. She hurried downstairs and found Greg in the main room, sitting in the shadows in the exact place where she had first seen him. He sat hunched over, his elbows braced on his knees—forehead resting on his upturned palms. He looked...defeated, Angelica decided.

"Are you okay?" she asked, her voice a whisper so as not to startle him. Concerned when he didn't answer, she flicked on the ancient wall sconces dotting the perimeter of the room. With the room washed in muted light, she could see blood stains on Greg's shirt and jeans. "What happened to you?" She rushed forward. "Where are you hurt?"

"*I'm* not," he said, his voice hoarse and barely above a whisper. "I'm sorry," he told her, then looked up, his eyes shadowed, haunted. "I was too late."

"Too late? Too late for what?"

"Adam Jones. He confronted them before I could

stop him. I found him shot in an alley not five doors from his house.''

''Confronted who exactly?''

''The Judges, I think. There was no gas leak. They'd opened the valves on an old propane canister in the basement. I'd noticed it when I looked the building over. It was on my list of things to handle, so it came into my mind earlier and I recognized the odor as propane. I imagine they hoped no one would identify the smell, since propane is so rarely used around here.''

Unable to deal with the full import of what Greg had said, she concentrated her thoughts on Adam. ''How is he?'' she asked, and regretted the quiver in her voice. Greg was suffering enough and didn't need to see how upset she was.

''He's in a coma.'' Greg's voice was flat. Emotionless. But that lack of emotion said just the opposite about his true feelings.

Angelica sat down next to him and put a comforting hand on his back. He stiffened at first, but then his muscles relaxed under her caress and he dropped his head back on his hands. She could feel every bone in his spine. He was still too thin.

''Greg, you did your best. You tried. You went after him to stop him, didn't you? You aren't responsible for Adam's choices. You can't do it all. Isn't that what you told me?''

''His parents showed up out of the blue,'' he went on, as if he hadn't heard her. ''They were getting out of their car. I didn't know who they were, so I asked them to see if Adam's parents were home. I told them he'd been hurt. What a way to find out your son's lying unconscious in an alley.''

"Will he be okay?"

"The trauma team says it's a waiting game now. If he makes it, he'll be fine in the long run. If he makes it.''

"Did he say anything about who shot him?"

"He was too worried about the gas problem here, and about Jean Ann. I think he was trying to tell me that the Judges were responsible for the gas. So I imagine that's who he confronted, and who shot him.'' Greg shrugged. "But he never said for sure or named anyone. After I told him everyone here was okay, he was more concerned with what would happen to him if he died. I was too busy answering those questions to push him about who shot him.''

"Were you able to lead him to the Lord?" At Greg's nod, Angelica felt peace close in around her soul. She knew without a shadow of a doubt that Adam would be fine whether he lived or died. But she knew—just *knew* with a definite certainty—that he would pull through. "Greg, that's so much more important than finding out who shot him.''

"Yeah. I thought so at the time," he said, defeated. But then he hesitated and shook his head. "No. I still do. Really.''

"Of course it is." She gripped his forearm and as she gave it a little reassuring squeeze, something electric zinged through her. Forcing herself to ignore it, she continued to minister to his soul. That was more critical than her own foolish attraction to him.

"For Adam, I know it is, but what about justice for Mr. and Mrs. Jones?" he asked.

"When he wakes up, and I promise you he will, Adam can tell the police who hurt him."

"If he wakes up," Greg corrected. "Don't get your hopes up."

She smiled. "Don't worry. He'll be fine. Don't ask how I know, but I know in my heart that he'll be fine. So tell me what happened next. After Adam accepted Christ."

"He tried to warn me about—" Greg sat up straighter, thinking. A frown creased his forehead. "I guess he meant the Judges, although he said 'judge'— in the singular. Maybe he sees them as one person— one threat to you and the mission."

"What did the police say? Did they question you?"

"Yeah. They said that if it was the Judges, they'd never be able to prove it."

"But maybe there are witnesses. Maybe somebody will come forward—"

Greg pursed his lips and shook his head. "Face it. Even if there is a witness, it will probably be someone who's also had trouble with the law and will be discredited if the case ever goes to trial."

"How can you be so sure?" she asked, curious again about his legal knowledge.

He sighed deeply, almost impatiently. "I just am. So unless Adam can ID the people who jumped him, an arrest isn't going to happen. And don't expect the police to work real hard on the case. It's just one street kid tangling with another as far as they're concerned. I told them Adam was a good kid, but they still didn't seem overly concerned about solving the mystery." Greg's eyes suddenly looked even more haunted. "If I'd only gotten there sooner."

Angelica frowned. "I thought we'd covered this ground. Why do you feel so guilty about this? You didn't even know Adam."

"Memories, I guess," he said absently, his voice quiet and his gaze far away, still tormented-looking. "Finding him brought back so many bad memories."

"Bad memories? Of the night you were shot?" He sat still as a statue, staring off into space. Some inner voice told her to push—probe. Make him face whatever haunted him. "Was there someone else hurt when you were?" she asked, having no idea where the thought had come from.

Greg looked up, startled. "What?"

"You said tonight brought back bad memories."

"I did?"

Angelica nodded. "And I asked if it was memories of when you were shot. Since you weren't hurt tonight, I guessed that it had to be memories of someone else being wounded."

Still staring straight ahead, he nodded after a few long heartbeats.

"And," she continued, knowing she had to prod him till he answered. Till he faced his demons. "I asked if there had been someone with you who was hurt, like Adam."

Greg stood suddenly and looked down at her, his eyes flashing with anger and more. So much more. There was a wealth of pain and other fierce emotion blazing there. Guilt, primarily. She was almost sorry now that she'd pried, except that she knew she'd had to do it. "She died in my arms. Is that what you wanted to hear? I couldn't save her, either!" he shouted. Then, as if he needed desperately to get away from the memories as much as he did her, he pivoted and stalked across the room and down the hall toward his room.

Could this be it, Lord? Could the death of the woman he'd spoken of be what put him on the streets? He's not responsible for her death, Lord, any more than he was for Adam's shooting. But he blames himself for both. Isn't that always the way? Show him, Lord. Teach him to lay his burdens at Your feet and not carry them on his own back. Help me to help him. Give him Your peace.

After a short phone conversation with Miriam Jones, Angelica felt anger, such as she had never before felt, begin to burn inside her. Then she had to break the news to Jean Ann. She woke the girl at dawn. Quiet and shaken, the teen accepted money for cab fare, then let Angelica put her in the taxi.

As she watched the bright yellow car weave its way up Rockland, Angelica felt the anger surge through her again. It was the kind of anger that her pastor had often called "righteous anger." She guessed Jesus had felt something akin to this when he'd found His father's house being defiled.

He had taken up a whip to drive out the money changers. Angelica knew she couldn't drive out the drug dealers and the rest of the Judges, but maybe she could rally the citizens to do something—anything—to show them that their misdeeds would no longer be blindly tolerated.

Angelica managed to rest on her bed for an hour, then showered and dressed. Still energized by her outrage, she sat at her desk and quickly outlined a plan, then went to seek out Greg. But not about her idea. Not yet.

She had thought long and hard, and planned to treat him as if nothing had happened between them in the small hours of the morning. As far as she was concerned, he had a right to his anger. She had pried. She wasn't sorry that she had, because she understood him better. But that didn't take away his right to take exception to having an open wound probed.

So minutes later, she strolled into the dining hall as if it were any other day. As if Greg Peters hadn't shouted his painful secret at her. As if she hadn't entered where angels fear to tread.

Angelica was nervous. Her heart pounded as she walked alongside the warming tray, scooping up a portion of scrambled eggs, some steamer-tray-soggy toast, and pouring herself a cup of coffee. She took a deep breath and turned, her gaze seeking Greg. For the first time, she was glad that her mother had forced her to learn to hide her feelings in public. She pasted on a neutral smile and made her way to the table where Greg sat.

"Good morning," she said, placing her tray across from his. She sat and dropped her napkin in her lap. "It's turned out to be another lovely day, hasn't it? I do so love these early summer days when the humidity is low, don't you?"

Greg looked up. "I'm sorry?"

Angelica managed to grit her teeth without losing the smile. All that and he'd been off in another world, she thought in disgust. "I said 'Good morning,' and then I commented on the lovely weather."

His gaze flitted around the room almost as if he'd

been unaware that it was morning at all. His eyes stopped searching when they reached the high windows. "Oh, the weather. Yeah. Nice couple of days."

"I always get more done on days like this."

"Yeah, so do I. I thought I'd clean out that basement today."

"That's a good idea. The men from the gas company came back for their fans and suggested we get rid of that propane canister. I guess it was left there from the building's days as a trade school."

"That makes sense. I want to check out the rest of the building to make sure there aren't any more accidents waiting to happen. It worries me that they put everyone here in danger with this latest incident. Breaking keys off in doorknobs and setting Dumpsters on fire was bad enough, but this latest stunt could have sent this place sky high, and taken everyone inside right along with it."

Angelica felt the anger boil up again. "It infuriates me, too. That and what they did to Adam. It's time for the residents to go on the offensive." Angelica picked up her fork to pretend great interest in her eggs, wondering what he'd say when he heard about her latest idea to bring North Riverside back to life.

"Are you crazy? These guys already have it in for you. You do anything else to stir things up and they'll be even more determined to get to you."

She smiled, knowing he'd given her his answer even though she hadn't asked the question. She'd print up and distribute the flyers first, then she'd tell him about the march. "The Lord will protect me, Greg. And if for some reason He chooses not to, then He must have another plan." She stood. "Well, I'll see you later. If you see Emanuel, tell him breakfast was grand.''

Greg stared at the sign tacked on the telephone pole. Surely, she hadn't done this. He read it aloud this time.

'''Take Back Your Streets. Join the staff of North Riverside Mission bright and early Saturday June 24th for a neighborhood cleanup. Or come later and join us for a candlelight march and prayer vigil. Starting point—NRM's front steps. Ending on Albert Street at the scene of the attack on Adam Jones. Come sing praise to the Lord and help cast out the evil from our midst. Sunday the 25th at one, the cleanup continues.'''

Greg tore the flyer down, stalked down the street and up the front steps of the mission. ''Where is she?'' he demanded when he found Manny using the copier in Angelica's otherwise empty office.

''Oh-oh. Guess you found one of the flyers.''

Greg noticed that Manny was reproducing even more of the things. ''She's really gone too far this time. They'll come after her for sure.''

Manny smiled a bit sadly. ''She knows no fear, my friend.''

''Well, I'm gonna talk some sense into that hard head of hers.''

''You can try, but you can't make her more afraid than she is mad. And you can't make her more afraid than she has faith. You have to learn that the Lord gives her the peace and courage to do these things.

She's doing this for the good of the neighborhood. What you ought to do is stay close to her—protect her from herself.''

Greg took a deep breath. Calmer, he nodded. "So where is she?"

"In the gym. I heard about a wild game of dodge-ball going on in there with the Vacation Bible School."

"VBS started yesterday?"

"Right on schedule. You've been around her long enough to know when she says something's going to happen, it will."

Yeah. Right. She never stopped, Greg thought. Just kept right on going. Like that darn pink bunny on the television commercial. But the bunny was no match for Judges, especially when they were crossed.

He needed to do something. But what? He couldn't order her as a police officer to stop the march. Nor could he do it on a personal level. All he was or could be to her was at best a friend or at least a helpful employee. So, as Manny suggested, he'd have to stick close by and watch out for her. Maybe it was a way to make up for his deception.

That decided, Greg pushed open the door to the gym and felt as if a hand had reached in his chest and squeezed his heart. Angelica was in the middle of two lines of neighborhood children, dodging a huge gym ball that had been fired directly at her. Her hair bounced in a high ponytail with her every move, and shone like fire in the sunlight. Eyes alight with joy, she goaded her youthful adversaries with loving teases. But it was ultimately what she wore that captured his gaze and held him frozen in place. They all had on shorts and a T-shirt, but the practical camp outfit on Angelica took his breath away. She had a trim figure that was delicate and feminine, and her dewy skin looked like silk. He longed to touch it.

She dipped to the left, avoiding yet another try at knocking her out of the game, and her musical laughter tinkled along his nerve endings. *Why her, Lord?* he asked for what was probably the hundredth time since meeting her. *Why do I have to feel so much for the one woman in the whole state who's going to hate me someday?*

"Greg," she called out, breathless and still laughing. "Come play. You look like you need to have some fun."

He looked at the flyer in his hand and shoved it in his back pocket. He shook his head, smiling in spite of himself.

Chapter Seven

"**A**ngelica," Greg called quietly, and knocked on the frame of her open office doorway. "Do you have a minute to talk? I really think you're—" But then the words clogged in his throat and the rest flew right out of his head. She looked up, as fresh from her shower as he was, her long hair still damp, curling in bright tendrils around her face, her green eyes still shining the way they had earlier while she'd played with the VBS kids.

Now, though she wore a modest dress in a pastel summery print, his memory filled in the blanks her camp outfit had revealed. And he knew with a sudden certainty that the attraction he felt for her wouldn't just go away the way it was supposed to—the way it always had with any other woman he'd met in the past six years.

Not now! his heart, his mind, his whole being cried. *I can't afford to care for her now!*

"Are you going to stand out there and talk to me?"

she was saying when her laughing question cleared the utter panic from his mind.

"Oh. No. I was just trying to decide how to—"

"How to talk me out of next weekend," she finished.

Greg raked his fingers through his hair, then dropped the hand in defeat. Why was he so transparent to this woman? "Well, yeah. Now that you mention it."

Her smile was almost blinding. "You aren't. It's too late. The neighbors—the ones on our side—are excited about it. All the local Scout troops and youth groups have called. They're helping organize the cleanup. All of the churches have called to lend their support. One of our corporate sponsors donated the help of a landscaper and his crew. The mayor even promised to send two city trucks to haul away the trash, and he's sending some anti-graffiti paint, too. It's mushroomed into something huge. It's the Lord, Greg. Whenever something grows like this, it's the work of the Lord. By Sunday morning there's going to be a tangible change in North Riverside. Whoever's behind all the trouble won't be able to deny what they see."

Hating to subdue her excitement even a little, but knowing someone had to be the voice of reason, Greg sat down in the chair across the desk from her. He had to point out the dangers. It was his job. But more pressing was a need he couldn't deny—a need to protect her. "And those people will have no further to look for someone to blame than 300 Rockland Street," he said. "Than this office. Than that apartment upstairs."

Her smile turned a bit sad. "And the Lord will protect me."

"The way he protected me? Or Jessie?" Greg spat out, and sucked in a shocked breath. Had that really come from him? Did he blame God for Jessie's death as much as he blamed himself? He looked down at his fisted hands.

Angelica saw the surprise in Greg's eyes before he cast his eyes downward. He was clearly shocked by his own revelation. But she wasn't. She stood, came around the desk and leaned back against it. "I'm sorry about your friend. And I'm sorry that the Lord had a different plan for your life and hers than either of you saw. But understand, Greg. He does have a plan for each of us—for you."

"I don't blame Him. I don't know why I said that."

"You probably said it because deep down that's how you feel. He understands and He's waiting to comfort you."

"I've tried to turn it all over to Him. But then she's there in my dreams, dying—and I can't stop it. The guilt. The pain. The anger. They all come right back. I should have been able to stop it. I don't understand why I couldn't. I'd been in that—" He cut off what he'd been about to say and looked up at her. "I've got to go." He stood.

Angelica wished it didn't hurt her—this love he obviously still felt for Jessie. But she accepted the pain as a gift. Because seeing the love and pain in his eyes when he'd talked of her death brought Angelica to a certainty that it was Jessie's death that had put Greg where he was now. "Greg, I'm here if you need

to talk. And about the activities for the weekend—I'd
appreciate your support even though you think I'm
being foolhardy.''

He stared down at her for a long charged moment,
then a slight smile tipped his lips upward on one side.
The lopsided grin made her heart turn over.

''I don't think anything of the kind. I think you're
incredibly brave and wonderfully true to your convic-
tions.'' The smiled slipped then. ''But so was Jessie.
I don't want to lose another—'' he stopped, then
spoke his next words hesitantly ''—another…
friend.''

''I can't make promises about the actions of others.
I can't even promise not to fall down the steps and
break my neck. All any of us can do is live our lives
and follow the Lord's lead no matter what circumstance the world puts us in.''

The smile came back to his lips, but it had that
faintly embarrassed quality to it that she always found
endearing. ''I guess you're right. That is all any of us
can do. Which means that you need my support, not
my criticism.''

She smiled then, too, and nodded, fighting the urge
to reach out and touch him. It was a need she didn't
fully understand. Because it wasn't a yearning to
comfort that made her want to hold him and be held
by him. It was a different kind of longing. And it
frightened her with its intensity.

''Then you've got my support,'' Greg said. ''Show
me what needs doing.''

Back behind the desk, and with Greg seated again,
she put the confusion and fear away for another time.
She sorted through her messages and papers and

quickly outlined a weekend that started at sunrise on Saturday and, except for some time to sleep and go to church, didn't stop until after dark on Sunday. It was ambitious—she knew that. According to the mayor, it was just short of revolutionary. That assessment seemed a little extreme to her. She chalked it up to political rhetoric.

Greg listened to the developing plans and wondered if anyone had ever tried anything so far-reaching on the North side before. If they had, he hadn't heard of it, and saw no evidence of it in the community. It would indeed be like waving a red flag in front of the troublemakers. He wished he weren't so sure that the local police couldn't be counted on to protect the workers and marchers. Even the support of the mayor wouldn't guarantee a peaceful day.

What they needed was the support of the whole city. And the only way to get that was the same way that the North side got all the bad press. They'd need to use the media to tell this story. And then just watch the Third Precinct try to turn a deaf ear toward the day's activities and the need for security! He might even be able to get the word out for some uniformed volunteers. It wasn't an answer to the problem of Angelica's long-term safety, but at least Saturday and Sunday would have a chance. And looking at the animated joy on her face as she explained the plans that had developed, he knew he had to throw his whole support behind her efforts.

"Let's give the television stations a call," he said. "And maybe WKBC. They're always running remote feed from events at the city's churches. This ought to be perfect for one of their community spots.''

"But you weren't even happy with the flyer we put out. I saw you looking at it in the gym before you stuffed it in your pocket and joined our games.''

"How did you—''

"Emmanuel made them a very distinct color so they'd be noticed. I noticed. The flyer *and* the look on your face when you looked down at it.''

Greg shrugged. "It isn't as if I don't think it's a good idea. I'm only worried about you. And since you're determined, the best way to make sure the weekend is a success is to force the police into making it a safe event. The press being there should take care of police apathy. And failing that, I think the Judges are too smart to pull something in front of the press and their cameras. They'd have to realize that any trouble they caused could make the governor mobilize his new anti-gang task force and send them in here.''

"I doubt it. I even asked Judge Whiting to contact the governor about getting them in here to look into the Judges. Nothing's happened.''

Greg was surprised, and it must have shown on his face.

"I really have tried to get help up here,'' she said defensively.

"Oh, I don't doubt it. I just can't understand the governor not seeing the problem here.''

She shrugged. "It may be worse in Philadelphia or Pittsburgh or somewhere else in the state. It's easy for those of us who live here to forget that there are others out there who may have bigger problems than we do.''

Greg stared at her through narrowed eyes. He needed to understand that about her. Why was she here and what was the cause of the estrangement from her family? He leaned forward and asked, ''Why do you live here? I know you come from another world. I asked once in anger, but I really would like to understand.''

''I felt God called me here. So I followed His wishes.''

''But what about your family? They must be worried about you.''

''They don't understand this,'' she said, gesturing to include the whole mission.

''And doesn't that bother you?''

''It used to. But now I just put their opinions out of my mind. I can't help or change the way they feel, so I try not to dwell on it. And nothing can change our mutual pasts. Maybe someday they'll understand and accept me and my work. I can only keep praying that they find the Lord, as I have.'' She pinched the bridge of her nose as if trying to ward off a headache.

''Are you all right?'' Greg asked. ''I didn't mean to bring up a painful subject.''

She shook her head and smiled, but it was forced. ''Don't be silly. I'm just building to a doozy of a headache. I should have gotten more sleep last night after getting none the night before.'' She checked her watch. ''In fact, if I go lie down now, I'll have enough time to take a nap before dinner. I'll contact the press tomorrow. Thanks for the idea.''

* * *

Greg watched her as she left, then, shaking his head in confusion, he went in search of a phone book. He wanted to call the local stations for her. If they could stagger the VHF, UHF and cable stations' coverage throughout the weekend, the Judges would never be without the threat of cameras. It took a couple of hours to coordinate the TV stations and contact WKBC, but by dinner hour he had the press coverage nailed down for her.

"This is wonderful. I can't believe you got them all to agree," she said, when he told her over dinner.

"It wasn't hard. Weekends are usually slow news days and this is a follow-up to a story about Adam that they've already covered." He thought of the young man, steadily improving but in slow increments, not yet conscious or able to identify his attackers. And he thought of the men out there who were a danger to the community—and Angelica—and he prayed for more ideas to make this project a safe one. "We just have to hope that nothing big happens to bounce us off the front page. Hey! Front page. We ought to call the papers, too!"

Angelica laughed. "And you tell me I get carried away. You'll have the press tripping over themselves."

"I staggered the times they're supposed to be here on Saturday, but the PBS station is talking about sending a crew here for the whole weekend. The woman I talked to even discussed the possibility of doing a documentary. It may not fly, but the camera will still be here and be a threat. It'd be a nice bonus toward getting funds in here, but it's gravy. And the three major networks will be here for the vigil on

Albert Street,'' he explained. Then he realized with a start that she was right. Greg grinned. He had gotten carried away. And it felt great!

Greg sat up in the darkness. This was ridiculous. He had to get some sleep, but Angelica filled his thoughts. He'd made her happy with the work he'd done today. And he'd made himself happy as well.

He remembered the feeling, but it had been years since he'd felt quite like that. Since Tommy's death. Since his graveside vow. Could it be that he hadn't been listening to the Lord, but to his own need for revenge? Wasn't he supposed to be a cop?

No, he told himself. That couldn't be it. He was just going through a bad spell. Maybe he just needed to get out of undercover work. He was getting too old for it, anyway. He'd gone from playing a high school kid looking for kicks, to pretending to be a mover and shaker on his undercover assignments. His successes had gotten bigger and more spectacular, but they were also more draining. And his failures were just plain dangerous and ultimately tragic. Jessie's death had shown him that. Now, recovering from her death and his own shooting, he had apparently been suited only to play a homeless bum.

At least until Angelica DeVoe had smiled down at him and offered her help. He was not so much a fool that he didn't understand that it had been Greg Peters, and not Detective Peterson, that she wanted to help. But her generous spirit had helped him just the same. He was still conflicted and confused, but since arriving at the mission at least he'd had a few moments of joy to give him hope and to remind him that there was another way to live.

Along with bringing him joy, she tormented him as well. He couldn't get her out of his head. But it wasn't her good works that obsessed him. It was her sunny smile. Her warm gaze. Her captivating laughter.

Greg rolled over and punched his pillow and rolled over again. *Come on Lord, I need some sleep here.*

The Lord answered his impatient prayer, but Angelica's laughter and smile and all the rest of his torturous thoughts followed him into sleep. Because you just can't outrun your destiny when it comes from Him.

Angelica finished her water and went back to her rumpled bed. She gazed toward the air conditioner in one of her windows, but she made no move to turn it on. She rarely used it. It was old and terribly inefficient. Besides, it was not the summer heat that wouldn't let her sleep.

It was Greg Peters.

And his question. And her memories. Angelica felt the same familiar knot form in her stomach that she always did whenever she thought of her family. Then her mind flashed back to her attraction to Greg and the reasons for it. She couldn't deny that he would be unsuitable in her father's eyes.

Was it Greg? Or was it rebellion?

Go away! I don't care what you think, she told her absent parents.

But the old scenes replayed. Had she ever stopped defying them? Angelica truly believed she had. After she'd come to Christ, she had gone to them and apologized for all her teenage rebellions. She had embraced them in love, even though they'd rejected and ridiculed her faith. But then they'd rejected her by stealing her money.

And Greg was... Well, he was just Greg. A caring man who had lost someone to violence and who had lost himself as well. One day, maybe with her help, he would be whole again.

Then he wouldn't be unsuitable at all, a voice whispered in her head, as sleep and visions of Greg claimed her mind and heart.

Chapter Eight

"Greg, am I going to get my office back any time soon?" Angelica asked, poking her head in her own office door.

Holding his index finger in the air, he begged for one more something—minute, call, hour? She didn't know, but he'd been on the phone all morning. And she still had no idea why. She knew it had to do with the cleanup weekend, but she still didn't know what.

She wasn't worried exactly. If Greg was involved, it would be something good. No, it was that she felt like a kid on Christmas Eve—knowing something great would be under the tree but dying to know what.

She sighed and turned to go back down the hall, when Greg called out, "Don't go. It's all yours. I have to go pick up the truck."

"Truck? What truck?"

He grinned. "The truck to use to pick up the paint."

"What paint?"

He laughed.

"Greg, start at the beginning." Angelica couldn't help smiling back at him. "You went to the hardware store after breakfast for a light switch, ran back in here, begged for my office, then tossed me out. What's going on?"

"It started at the hardware store. They had this stack of paint cans that they were moving to their Dumpster. But they looked heavy. You know, like they were full. And it turns out that they were. Apparently they mix custom paint. If it doesn't come out right, they play with it, but if they can't get it right, they start all over and toss out the first gallon.

"So I talked to the owner. He said all paint stores and the big chains do the same thing."

"So you've been calling *all* of them?"

His grin widened and started looking smug. "All over the city."

"So now we have to rent a truck to pick it all up?"

Angelica noticed his eyes shift away. "Not exactly. I got one donated for the afternoon."

"From who?"

He shrugged carelessly, but the twinkle in his blue eyes made her think of the proverbial cat with a scent of canary on his breath.

"What?" she said.

He just smirked in answer.

Angelica put her hands on her hips and stood over the desk, looking down at him. "There's something you should know about me. I love surprises—unless I know there's going to be one. Then I'm merciless. I have to know. Christmas was torture for me. I almost hated it!"

Greg laughed. It seemed to swell from the center of his being and spill out. He'd laughed before in amusement at one of the children, or in cheerful camaraderie with her or Emanuel, but this was unadulterated joy ringing from him. It sounded wonderful and free.

She caught her breath as her heart seemed to swell in her chest. For him. For the sound of happiness and the look of it shining from his eyes.

"Tell me, or I'll have Emanuel serve you... ketchup soup for lunch," she threatened. It wasn't much, but it was the best threat she could come up with on short notice.

Still laughing, he held up his hands as if to ward off an attack. "No. No. Not the dreaded ketchup bottle. Stop. Please. No more. I'll talk."

"You'd better," she warned him, and sat in the chair he usually occupied when they talked in her office. It seemed strange to see someone else in her place, but not as awful as she might once have thought. The Lord and the mission had been at the top of her list of priorities for two years, but now Greg seemed to belong there as well. Ahead of North Riverside Mission.

Greg, she noticed suddenly, was staring at her. Flustered, hoping her thoughts hadn't been reflected on her face, she said, "So tell me!"

He blinked. "Okay. Remember we talked about Homes for Restoration and the problem with the banks? So when I was at Josey's, the head of their local effort was there, and I talked to him. He said that they were working on a new idea to help in the upkeep of existing homes where the owners didn't have enough money to do repairs. It would work the same with everybody pitching in, but with the money coming from straight donations. The hope being that if they got existing homes spruced up and therefore the housing values went up, the banks would begin to see the value of the neighborhood.

"So I called him about the 24th. He lent me their truck for the rest of the day. And…"

"And?" she coaxed when he drew out the suspense.

"And they're lining up volunteers for the weekend to show up with scrapers, paintbrushes, rollers and the rest of what they'll need. It'll be what they call a 'blitz.' They work like crazy until all the supplies are gone. And Homes for Restoration is going to try getting some repair supplies donated as well."

Angelica couldn't believe it. "Wow! When you get going, you don't stop."

Greg shook his head. "Nope. You said it yesterday. It's the Lord. Nothing falls together like this unless He's the reason."

Greg thought about that at dawn on Saturday as workers began to gather in the big yard behind the mission. By seven, they had signed in and were assigned tasks. Besides local residents, there were almost five hundred of them, thanks to a little advance publicity by one of the TV stations and Homes for Restoration. And nearly every store had donated more than just their discarded interior- and exterior-grade paint cans. Between those supplies and the truckload Restorations had arrived with, he wondered how anyone could fail to see God's hand at work.

"Pinch me," Angelica said, as she looked over his shoulder at the clipboard where the volunteers had signed in.

"I know what you mean." He handed her the clipboard. "I hope you don't mind that I let the guys from Homes for Restoration pretty much take charge. They've had so much experience organizing teams that it seemed like a waste of time to reinvent the wheel."

Angelica laid her hand on his arm. He had to fight not to let the muscles beneath her hand tense. "Who does what doesn't matter," she told him. "Getting it done does. I wanted to let you know that Joe Conway is in town to make final preparations for their July Jam Crusade. He called to ask if we wanted him to direct a church service here in the morning. I wasn't sure how many people would come, but he said that wherever two or more are gathered in His name, He's there. So he's coming, no matter how few attend. Jean Ann's inside, running off some half-sheet flyers to hand out to the workers.

Greg smiled. He had another surprise for her. "We can tuck the flyers in their lunches."

"Lunches?"

"The WKBC crew pulled in a few minutes ago. I told them they could set up around front under the oak. Anyway, one of the burger places called them. They're sending over lunches. All they wanted in return was for the DJ to mention that they'd done it."

Tears welled up in Angelica's eyes, reminding him of field grass after a spring rain. "Oh dear," she said shakily, and bit her lip.

Grabbing his handkerchief, he caught the tears as

they fell. "Hey, hey. What's this?" he crooned. "You'd think no one showed up. Instead, we're seeing a miracle happening right here in River City."

She gave him a watery smile. "I'm not sad. I'm happy."

"Oh, I get it. My mom does that over the dumbest things."

"You have a mother?" she asked.

"No," he said in a serious tone. "I was hatched at the local zoo." He laughed at the look of chagrin that passed over her face. "Come on. We're assigned to that vacant lot on Stewart with the landscaping crew. They were trying to decide whether to turn it into a park, a playground or a big victory garden. But first, it's full of trash."

She looked up at him, her eyes shining in the sunlight. "I need my work gloves. I'll be right back."

Greg watched her take off at a run, then stop and turn back to him. She tilted her head and just looked for a long moment, then, with a shake of her head, she was off again. That was another close one. He had to remember to guard his tongue around her; right now he was Greg Peters, not Detective Gregory Peterson, and Peters was alone in the world. Peters hadn't had anywhere to go when she'd met him.

Unfortunately, someday soon she would feel betrayed by both of them.

Greg walked briskly down Central Street and turned left on Beech as instructed. He looked around once more, just to make sure he hadn't been followed. Then he spotted Jim Lovell, leaning against his car in front of DelAssandro's.

As Greg came even with the car, Jim stood up and motioned him inside the restaurant. He followed, and a minute later stepped into a small room to the left of the kitchen. The lone occupants of the room—Captain Torres, Jim Lovell's boss, and Greg's boss, Captain Glen Harris—sat in a booth.

"We've got to stop meeting like this," Greg quipped as he settled into the booth across from Torres and Harris. He tossed an envelope full of evidence between them. Torres reached for it.

"Peterson, cut the comedy," Harris growled. "Mind telling me what your face was doing plastered all over the news last night?"

Greg looked at all three men. "I couldn't very well have put my hands in front of my face. Besides, the image was blurred from what I saw. He was shooting Angelica and she was several feet in front of me."

"Still, you could have endangered yourself and your cover. I recognized you. You've been about ten different people in the last six years. Suppose someone else recognized you?"

"I was in the background of a public event. So what if they did? If I'd done anything to avoid being photographed, it would have made people suspicious."

Harris sighed. "I hope you're right. You aren't even fully recovered from your last bout with a bullet. I don't want anyone using you for target practice again."

"I know I took a chance having the press there, but it was the only way I could think of to protect the volunteers. It was a cinch that the Third couldn't be counted on."

"Well, just be careful in the future, will ya?"

Greg nodded. "Sure, Captain."

"He's worried about your health, but I'm worried about my investigation," Torres said. "Keep off TV, Peterson. I don't want anything to go wrong. I want these dirty cops turned up and fast."

"So do I. They're a threat to Angelica."

"There's no evidence against her in here," Captain Torres said as he rifled the papers Greg had given them.

Greg took a deep breath. He knew he was too close to this, and losing his temper wouldn't help matters. "That's because she is exactly what she appears to be—an innocent civilian trying to make our jobs easier by turning that neighborhood around. There's nothing in the envelope because there's no evidence to find. You didn't hear anything in the least compromising in the surveillance tapes, did you?"

"Nothing," Harris agreed.

"I didn't think so," Greg said. "Look, the threats against her are becoming serious." Once again, he outlined the three recent incidents that had all been in his reports, ending by tying the problem with the propane gas to the shooting of Adam Jones. Adam was still in a coma. And things had been quiet around the mission for over a week. Too quiet.

"All right, Peterson. Point taken," Harris said.

Greg saw a ray of hope. "I want out of the buying. Every buy I make jeopardizes funding at the mission. Angelica is an innocent caught in a web of police corruption. If she has to close down, we may as well hand that neighborhood over to the gang and the Third Precinct. We can't continue to put Angelica

DeVoe's work at risk. I want to pull the bugs, as well.'' He pushed himself up straight, ready for a fight, but was surprised by the response he got.

Harris nodded. ''I was going to tell you to lay off the buys for now, anyway. You look ragged around the edges. Fix broken stuff at that mission and watch for anything suspicious. And you can tell her who you are if it becomes necessary to protect your cover. You got a problem with that, Torres?''

Torres shook his head. ''No. You can also pull the surveillance equipment, and I'll pull the truck. I can't waste any more man-hours on tapes of counseling sessions and kids playing. Like your captain, I didn't think the bugs were necessary after you first vouched for her. I'd like to thank you, Detective Peterson, for what you've done. I know it isn't easy to turn in fellow officers on possible bribery charges, and it certainly won't be a popular decision for you to have made, once this is out.''

Greg nodded. ''It's the right thing to do. After getting to know the people being hurt by them, it is easier to do than I'd thought. Can I unload the marked bills with you guys now, since I can stop making buys? I have about seven hundred left and I brought it along.''

Torres shook his head. ''Keep the cash for now. You may have to pick up with the buys again. We're setting up a sting operation to see if the Third is just taking bribes, or if they're actively involved in the drug operation itself.''

''How did we get from some uniforms possibly taking bribes to look the other way and mess with evidence all the way to police officers supplying drugs?'' Greg wanted to know. Had to know. Maybe they'd found the evidence that Greg had been looking for.

Jim spoke up. "Worth, one of the two you tangled with in the Jackson arrest, has a girlfriend who works in Central Evidence. I saw him hanging around there, and I got to thinking about a few things.

"You were put in the mission because someone tipped us to what was supposed to be Angelica DeVoe's involvement in trafficking. But you told us she was innocent and that some of her funding had been endangered because you were her employee and you'd been seen with a dealer.

"Suppose she'd been openly accused or even brought in for questioning. That place would have gone under in weeks—days, maybe. Right?''

Greg nodded. "That's what I've been saying all along.''

"You also said Angelica DeVoe is making life tough for the Third and the Judges. So the tip probably came from that quarter. She's not the supplier, but somebody is, because we *do* know the problem in that area really is drugs. And the Third keeps turning up like a bad penny. And Worth is with the Third.

"So I checked Central Evidence. Sometime in the last two months, drugs being held there have been replaced with benign substance. It's been two months since you dried up that big syndicate down by the wharfs. But drugs are still coming in from somewhere.''

Torres chimed in. "We don't want to tip our hand by questioning the girlfriend, so we'll have to take a more circuitous route. Thus, the sting I mentioned.

When we're ready to take them all down, we'll pull her in and offer to plead her down in exchange for her cooperation.''

"How will you go about the sting?'' Greg asked.

Harris picked up then. "We're setting up a phony lab in an abandoned house in North Riverside on Oak. The narcotics team, sans you and a few other undercovers, will lead a raid. But we'll ask for uniformed help from the Third. We won't catch anyone there, of course, but we'll confiscate and store the drugs at the Third in their drug locker. The product will already be marked. With no perps taken in the raid, they'll know it'll never be called up as evidence and eventually will be destroyed. That ought to make them feel real comfortable about making use of it.''

"Is that when I get involved again?''

"Yeah,'' Harris said. "I've put Turner and Bradock in the neighborhood. They've moved into that apartment house on Maple. But at that point you need to pick up the buys again. We don't want too many new faces showing up in the neighborhood, looking for a connection. You've become known, so it isn't likely that anyone would be suspicious of you.''

Greg felt sick. They wouldn't have come up with such an elaborate scheme if they weren't convinced that they were right. "You really think the Third's helping supply the Judges?''

His expression grim, Torres nodded. "But we need the marked drugs to show back up on the streets, and we need to prove where they came from. Any product going into Central Evidence will be marked as well, and hidden cameras have been installed. We'll let you know if anything disappears from there. That's about it for now," he finished, glancing down at his watch. "I've got a meeting with the commissioner in half an hour, and he doesn't like to be kept waiting."

"Greg, I'll drop you back closer to the North side," Lovell offered as the two police captains stood.

Jim Lovell held back, watching as the older men left. "You can trust them," he told Greg as he slid out of the booth and back in to sit across from him. "Torres is as honest as they come. And I checked out Harris. I didn't like the way he sent you into this situation so soon after you got back on duty. The most you should have been doing was stakeouts for a few months. But he did check out. He asks a lot of his people, but no more than he's given in the past himself."

"I know. I'd trust Captain Harris with my life. Don't forget this was *supposed* to be a simple assignment."

"But it's anything but simple, and it's tearing you apart."

"No," Greg said, shaking his head. "It's been tough in a lot of ways, but it's been good for me, too. Believe it or not, I've had time to start reevaluating things."

"What things?"

Greg shrugged. "The things I talked about last time I saw you. Who I am. My relationship with the Lord."

Jim Lovell frowned. "I didn't know that was a problem. I thought that was the one thing that kept you going most of the time."

"It was. It *is*. But as I said last time, I've been undercover so long that I've lost something, too. I don't know what's wrong yet, but at least now I'm closer to understanding what's missing—what I lost somewhere along the line."

"Greg, you're supposed to be on an assignment," Lovell said, his voice tight and intense, "not examining the state of your life and your soul. This is exactly what I've been worried about."

"I'm fine," Greg promised, but knew he very well might not be. He understood Jim's worry. His mind wasn't solely on his work these days.

"No, you're not fine. You're exhausted, for one thing."

Greg scrubbed his hand over his face. "Yeah. I'm tired. But since I don't have to go out nights anymore, I'll be fine."

Jim had perfected an indignant scowl by age ten, and the expression had only become more eloquent. "So you did get all that evidence and information at night."

"You'd be surprised how alive the streets are at three and four," he told his friend with an insolent grin. "And it's easier to follow someone when there are shadows to blend in with. Plus, I didn't need to lie about where I'd been if I could sneak out after everyone was in bed."

"And will you have to lie when you get back today?"

Greg grimaced. "That depends on how busy things have been for Angelica, and on how busy the place is when I get back."

"And lying to her has become a problem?"

"Yeah, it has. I haven't even been entirely honest with you guys, either. I had information from an informant that the Third was more involved with the drugs than turning their backs, but I didn't say anything.''

''Because you didn't have any proof, and because of who Rossi is to Donovan.''

Greg nodded. ''And because you don't accuse another officer when there's doubt left in your own mind. I couldn't get proof of anything other than their obviously bad procedure.''

''Okay. I understand why you kept it to yourself. What makes you think Angelica won't be as understanding as me?''

''She has a problem with being lied to—a big problem with it. I have a bad feeling about how she'll react when she finds out her trust in me has been misplaced.''

Jim was incredulous. ''She'd rather you were a street person than an honest, hardworking undercover police officer?''

Greg shook his head. ''She wants me to get my life back together. The issue is going to be that I lied, not who I am. And don't forget, I was originally there to spy on her. I've searched and bugged the building. Even her apartment.''

''Are you in love with her?''

Greg wished he could deny it, but he truthfully didn't know the answer. ''I hope not, because I'll lose her over this.''

''So tell her before she finds out some other way. They gave you the go-ahead if it was necessary. As far as I'm concerned, it's necessary if it gives you one less distraction. Just tell her. If you don't get your mind on business, you're going to make a dangerous mistake.''

"Like I did with Serinto?"

"Greg, that was Jessie's mistake—and you know it. She was the one who blew her cover, and yours along with it."

"But I was the one in charge of the operation." Greg shook his head. "She blew our cover a full week before it all went bad at that warehouse. I should have seen that they were leading us into a trap."

"From what I hear, you did suspect a problem. You told Harris that something didn't smell right, and he had more men on the warehouse than he normally would. Including a couple of sharpshooters. Neither Serinto nor any of his men got away that night. You and Jessie took down one of the biggest drug rings Riverside ever had, and you took it out from the top down. There was no one left to resurrect their syndicate."

"And Jessie still died!" Greg suddenly saw the pain that had invaded Jim's eyes. He felt stupid and selfish for his outburst. Jim was the one person he shouldn't have talked to about this.

"Yeah." Jim swallowed deeply. "Jessie still died, but her death did mean something. She died making a difference."

"But I was the one who asked for her. I dragged her into that particular battle."

"And she nearly got you killed. Her mistake. She was thinking about something else. Someone else. You think I don't know that?" Jim paused. He glanced down at the floor, then back to Greg. "It was me she was in love with. It was probably me she was thinking about—not you. So maybe it was my fault. Did you ever think of that?''

No, Greg never had. Maybe because he'd been so busy blaming himself. Why hadn't he realized it before now?

Chapter Nine

Angelica gripped the phone more tightly. "Mother, I did not stage last weekend's activities in North Riverside just to embarrass you and Father. It was just what it looked like on the news. A lot of neighbors and volunteers getting together to pray and to contribute to a community betterment project. It was very successful."

Her mother sniffed. "If you paint a mausoleum, there are still rotting bodies inside."

Even after a moment's thought, Angelica was at a loss. "What on earth is that supposed to mean?"

"You're the one always reading and quoting the Bible. I would think you'd understand a biblical reference when you hear one. I mean that those people in North Riverside are the dregs of humanity, and will remain just that no matter how hard you work and no matter what their homes look like. They are inferior and nothing will make them any more."

Angelica shook her head, understanding at last. Her

mother was truly to be pitied. "The quote about 'whited sepulchers' referred to people who think they are better than everyone else."

"I should have known you would try to turn this around so we were in the wrong. You hate us and are still trying to punish us for removing that money from your account."

"It isn't my place to punish you. I think I was rather generous in not going to the police about what you and Father did," Angelica informed her mother coldly. "Had I wanted you punished, I would have created a scandal that would have driven Father's precious name straight into the ground."

"No, you would rather drag out our punishment."

Angelica gritted her teeth. "I am not trying to punish you! And I don't hate you. I just can't forgive what you did." Not that she hadn't tried, as she knew full well.

"You simply cannot make me believe that you forgot that your sister was due to make her debut last weekend."

"I didn't forget. I never knew about it. How would I? I don't read the society page anymore, so if it was announced there, I missed it. And I certainly didn't receive an invitation."

"As if you would have darkened our door!"

"You're right, Mother." Angelica pressed the heel of her hand to her forehead and took a deep breath. "I wouldn't have come, and I wasn't hinting that I should have been invited. I was merely pointing out that I had no way of knowing. I haven't heard from anyone in the family for more than a year. And since I couldn't possibly have known, I couldn't have staged last weekend's activities to coincide with her party."

"You were the talk of the evening."

Angelica took a deep breath and tried to fight off an approaching headache. "Tell Tracy that I'm very sorry if I stole her thunder. You should have told her to use my activities to explain my absence. She could have pretended to be proud of what I'm trying to do down here, instead of acting embarrassed by it."

"You live in a slum. You mix with degenerates. We *are* embarrassed."

"I fail to see why my efforts among the poor would embarrass any of you."

"Oh! No, I don't suppose you do. Goodbye, Angelica. I don't know why I waste my time trying to get you to come to your senses."

The phone slamming in her ear pushed Angelica over the edge, her head pounding with a full-blown headache. "I don't know either, Mother. I really don't," Angelica said shakily as she put the phone in its cradle. It rang again before she took her hand away. Prepared for more unpleasantness from one of her parents, she wearily picked it up again. "North Riverside Mission," she said.

The voice was young, but the message was as old as Cain. "You're gonna die, lady."

Angelica hung up the phone before the voice had a chance to add the usual foul names, or to embellish the threat. And her spirits plummeted. Everything had been going so well. Why did something always try to steal her joy? A problem. A tragedy. A threat.

The streets were free of litter for the first time in years. Anti-graffiti paint covered surfaces that had tainted the community with tag-names, foul language and ugly slogans. There was a new park on the sight of a torn-down factory. Flowers grew around the surviving sycamores that had once lined the streets. Vacant houses had been tightly sealed and spruced up. Fresh paint gleamed on the homes of those who had asked for help. People had hope of a better day.

Then her mother had called her for the first time in a year. But she hadn't called to beg forgiveness for her part in the underhanded theft of Angelica's legacy from her grandmother. She had called to berate her "wayward" daughter, once again. Angelica put her head down on her desk cushioned by her forearm, fighting tears that came no matter how hard she fought them.

"Angelica? What's wrong?"

Angelica looked up at Greg through a sheen of tears. She bit her lip, trying to get a hold on her runaway emotions, but the tears overflowed and tracked down her cheeks. "I just get tired sometimes, I guess. I get so tired of nasty phone calls and broken pipes and being alone. My mother called for the first time in a year. It seems I've embarrassed my family— again."

Greg grimaced and sat near her on the edge of her desk. "Some people just don't get it, do they?" He pulled out one of what seemed like an endless supply of handkerchiefs, took her chin in his strong hand, and dried her tears.

She looked up at him and wondered how someone so big and masculine could be so gentle with children and upset...friends. "I'm sorry. This is ridiculous. It was the two calls right in a row, I guess."

"Two calls?" Greg frowned. "What was the second?"

She shrugged and looked away, not wanting him to see how much this particular threat had shaken her. "Another stupid threat," she answered as casually as she could.

"What kind of threat?" Greg asked. His tone said she hadn't fooled him for a second.

"The same kind of thing. I hung up before he had a chance to get foul."

Greg laid his hand on her shoulder. "What exactly did he say?"

"I'm going to die. It isn't exactly news. We all are," she told him, trying for the flippant tone that she knew he would have used if it had been a threat against him.

Greg wasn't distracted, however. "I'm not going to let anything happen to you, Angel."

Only her grandmother had ever called her Angel. It touched a chord in her that said "love." The nickname and something in his tone dragged her gaze to meet his. What she saw in the depth of his blue eyes overwhelmed her. It said that he cared. Deeply. It said that the friendship he'd claimed was too nonchalant a word for what he felt toward her. It said there was a chance for them, because the emotions she'd been feeling were not all on her part. And there was an unyielding determination to keep his promise of protection written on the rest of his features, as well.

"Thank you," she said, believing in him. Believing in possibilities. She took a deep breath, feeling immeasurably better. Maybe his memories of Jessie wouldn't keep them apart, after all. Maybe Greg had found his way back to himself through the mission.

Through her dream.

Her dream for the people of North Riverside! The Judges wanted to destroy her dream. Destroy her people. "They make me so mad—those cowards!" The words exploded from her.

He chucked her playfully on the chin and grinned his marvelous crooked grin. "Hey! Now there's the spirit." But then the grin slipped. "But don't let that spirit make you do anything reckless. Please, don't go anywhere alone for a while. If you need to go somewhere, let me know, and I'll tag along, or Manny can if I'm in the middle of something. If we're both tied up, wait. Nothing's as important as your safety. Okay?"

"I didn't hire you or Emanuel as bodyguards."

"And see what a good administrator you are?" he said, grinning again, his blue eyes sparkling, yet tender. "You got a two-for-one deal with both of us."

She sighed. "Okay. I promise. And in that case, would you go with me to see Mrs. Jones? She asked me to stop by this afternoon. She wants to talk about Adam."

"Then we'll go over and talk. Come on."

There was no warning. One second, they'd entered the hallway, the sun streaming in the high overhead windows. The next, jagged shards of glass rained down. Angelica heard Greg shout her name. She had the vague impression that he tried to protect her with his body, but by then blackness had begun to fall as if something had blotted out the sun.

* * *

Greg stepped into the hall just behind Angelica, and turned to pull her office door closed. He whirled in the direction of a shattering noise from overhead. Horrified to see an object and a shower of glass falling toward Angelica, he called her name and dove for her. He pulled her against him and rolled to protect her from the hard terrazzo floor, then rolled again, cupping the back of her head and hovering over her to shield her from the still-falling glass. But even as the glass stopped raining down, he was aware that she was too limp in his arms. An unspeakable terror rose in his heart.

"Angel," he said in a choked voice that he barely recognized as his own. She didn't answer. He pushed himself away from her, falling to his side, while keeping her head cupped in his other hand. Glass fell to the floor from his back, and footsteps raced their way. But Greg could only stare into her too-lax features. He could feel her breathing against him, but she was otherwise, frighteningly still. She had taken a hard blow to her head and was bleeding, as well.

Greg moved as if in a nightmare, watching his actions as if from outside himself. He gathered Angelica into his arms and stood, getting help for her his only thought.

"Is she all right?" he heard Manny ask, as he and Antonio Ortiz ran toward them.

"No. Get her car started. Jean Ann, call St. Alfonso's. Tell them I'm coming in with her. Tell them she's unconscious." He looked down at the floor. "It was a brick. I think it hit her."

Jean Ann, white-faced, nodded and said, "She's out cold."

He shifted Angelica in his arms, leaning her head against his chest. He looked down and saw the gash at the crown of her head. "Somebody bring a clean towel and some ice to the car right away."

"Don't worry so. Head wounds bleed a lot," one of the women said, as he raced for the car. He climbed in the back seat, and someone pressed the towel and ice against Angelica's head. He held it in place and vaguely thanked whoever had brought it.

The ride was interminable. The only thought running through his mind was, *Please, God, don't take her away from me.* He repeated the litany hundreds of times but it remained the only thought his fear-engulfed mind could process.

Angelica heard voices at the end of the dark tunnel. They were muffled, but she recognized one. Greg. She moved forward, needing to find him. The darkness frightened her, and she knew with him nearby her fear would vanish. If she could just find him... But as she got closer to his voice, her head began to pound viciously. She dreaded the pain more than the blackness, so she let the voices fade and the darkness thicken again.

The next time Angelica heard Greg's voice, it came from much nearer, and there was light on the other side of her eyelids. But the pain in her head made her shy away from the light. All she had to do, she told herself, was open her eyes, and she'd see him. It was suddenly vitally important that she see him. Feel his touch. Touch him.

"I want to stay with her," Greg said, an edgy urgency in his tone. "Come on, Brian. What can it hurt?"

"There are rules. You aren't her husband. You sure aren't next of kin. You always used to think rules were important."

"Bry, there are threats against her. I can't leave, but I can't stay in an official capacity. Since when are you such a stickler for rules?"

"Since I grew up, big brother. Maybe you haven't been around enough to notice."

"I'm sorry I couldn't be there for you much. But I couldn't be. You know that. I had to do what I did. Mom and Dad understand that."

"Do they?" the other voice, the man he'd called Brian, asked. "Or do they just love you in spite of it all? Do you think they don't worry? They've lost one son already. Do you think the phone can ring late at night without it scaring them half to death? Have you got a clue what your getting shot did to them? It was the culmination of all their nightmares. Dad spent those first three days, while you were unconscious, popping nitro left and right. I was afraid I'd have to admit him, too."

Greg let out a strained sigh.

It was an anguished sound that made Angelica fight harder to reach him. But then her perceptions began to sharpen. The conversation began to make sense. Greg had family. A brother. Parents. Living nearby. Why had he not turned to them in his pain over Jessie? Why had he been out of their lives for so long that he hadn't realized his younger brother had become an adult?

"They didn't let me see any of that," Greg explained after a long pause. "When I came to, they seemed fine. All I saw was their love. All I felt was their support. Lately, I've realized I've been living in the shadows so long that I'm not seeing things clearly anymore. I guess I didn't see what a strain I'm putting on them."

"Go see them," Brian urged. "They need to see that you're all right. But, get a haircut, and shave off that sad excuse of a beard before you do. Or is there a reason for it?"

Greg's brother sighed, and Angelica supposed it was in response to some silent answer from Greg. "Well, at least call them."

"I'll call. Maybe I'll get out there and see them on my next day off."

"Good. Now back to Ms. DeVoe. You aren't next of kin and I'm not supposed to let you stay—but okay. Is she something to you other than—?"

"Yeah. I think so. But as you can imagine, it isn't that simple. When you get the time, pray for me, will you? I really need to get my head straight about why I'm doing all this. I—I'm not sure anymore."

"Greg, nothing's been simple with you since Tommy died." Brian frowned. "It wasn't your fault."

"I wish I could make myself believe that."

"Try, will you? I've lost one brother. I don't want to lose another."

Material rustled, and she heard Greg settle close by, but Angelica still couldn't get her eyes open. "Greg," she said. It took a lot of effort, but she did indeed hear her own voice whisper into the room.

"Hey. Decide to join the world again?" He took

her hand, touched her cheek and brushed some hair off her forehead. Nothing had ever felt so wonderful.

"Um. I can't seem to get my eyes open, and my head hurts like crazy. What happened to me? Where am I?"

The hand holding hers tightened a bit. "Don't worry about that now. Just open those pretty green eyes and look at me."

Somehow the yearning in his voice gave Angelica the strength she needed. She fought the pain and forced her heavy eyelids to open. Greg's image swam before her for a couple of seconds, then she was able to focus on his face. He stood next to her, looking more than just worried. He looked terrified.

"Am I in a hospital?" she asked.

"Yeah, Angel, you're in a hospital."

"Did I have an accident?"

"Yeah. You got hurt." His voice shook.

"Do I hear conversation in here?" the man she'd heard before asked.

"She woke up," Greg told the young blond man advancing toward the bed. When he grinned, it was with Greg's grin, but not with the crooked lift to one side that she loved. Greg had called him...Brian.

"O, ye of little faith. I told you she would," Brian said. "Now, Ms. DeVoe, I'd like to get a good look at you. You, out," he told Greg.

Greg's jaw stiffened. "I'm not leaving. I'll stand outside the curtain, but I'm *not* leaving."

"Greg has an overdeveloped sense of responsibility for others, in case you haven't noticed," Brian quipped. "Now can you squeeze my fingers?" he asked, wrapping her fingers around his middle and index fingers.

She squeezed his fingers, pushed against his hands with her hands and feet, followed his too-bright light, and performed various other tasks that he explained would show possible neurological damage.

"Do you want Greg back in here, Ms. DeVoe?" he asked once his exam was done.

"Yes," she answered automatically.

"Greg, come on. Your pacing's going to drive the staff crazy. You have a concussion," he told Angelica, looking no less young for his apparent competence as a doctor. "But you should be feeling fine in a few days. A cut on your head, a couple on your arm, and one on your leg have been stitched. You should wait a few days before showering, and come back in ten days to have your stitches removed. Or you can go to your own doctor, of course."

"Can I go home now?" That was all she wanted to know.

Angelica hated hospitals. The smell brought back the long, painful days leading to the loss of her beloved grandmother—the only family member who'd understood her faith in Jesus and had embraced Him. They had been bittersweet days when she alone sat waiting for her grandmother to go home to be with the Lord, where all pain would be gone. But on that day she'd lost her best friend. Little had she known how absolutely alone in the world she would feel.

"I'd like to keep you overnight for observation," Brian said.

"No. I won't sleep a wink here," Angelica protested. "I want to go home. No offense, but I hate hospitals."

He turned to Greg. "She could go home if someone were there to watch over her and wake her every hour through the night."

"I'll be there to take care of her. What about tomorrow? Any restrictions as far as work?"

"Rest for a day or two, preferably longer. I'd prefer she stick to acetaminophen or ibuprofen for the pain because of the head injury. And I'll see *you* in ten days to take out the stitches in your arm." Brian looked back to Angelica and grinned. Anyone would pick them out as brothers. "This is probably the first time in his life that my brother hasn't passed out from a bad cut. He didn't even know he was bleeding until one of the nurses noticed. Fear is a great way to raise someone's blood pressure."

"Doctor, the patient in Three is worse," a woman said, looking into the small examination room.

"Well, duty calls," Brian said. "Take care, both of you. The nurse'll be in with discharge papers in a few minutes. She'll help Ms. DeVoe get dressed."

"That's your brother," Angelica said.

"You—ah...heard us?"

"Mmm, hmm. He sounds as if he really cares about you." She really looked at him for the first time. "You look awful."

Greg pushed his hair out of his eyes. "I was worried about you. I was so worried. I'm sorry."

"Sorry? You don't look that bad."

He shook his head. "Sorry that you got hurt."

"Was my accident your fault?"

"It was no more an accident than the rest of what's

been going on. Somebody threw a brick through the hall window. I tried to keep you from getting hurt, but I was too late.''

''You didn't throw the brick,'' she said mildly.

He glared at her. ''Very funny. Of course, I didn't throw the brick.''

She tried to smile at his indignation, but she felt sad that he always seemed to feel responsible for the ills of the world. ''Then how is my being hit by it your fault?''

''I promised to protect you.''

She did smile a little then, hoping to make him feel better. ''You can only try your best. You can't see the future and into the hearts of men. You can't be everywhere. You aren't God, Greg.''

''I know what you're saying. It's just—''

''That's the only way you could have prevented this,'' she cut in. ''Face it. No one could have stopped this, except whoever threw that brick.''

Greg smiled. ''You're incredible. You know that?''

Did he think she was too good for him? Had she unconsciously sent him some sort of signal ingrained in her by her pretentious family? Hadn't she even weighed his suitability by her parent's standards at first? ''I'm nothing special, Greg. I sin. I make mistakes. Don't put me on a pedestal. I don't deserve it.''

Gazing into her luminous eyes, Greg's heart felt about to burst with all that he yearned to say to this beautiful, wonderful woman. But he didn't have the right, did he? Not until she knew the truth about him.

While he pondered this problem, the nurse who'd called Greg's brother away breezed in. ''So, are you all ready to get on your way?''

Chapter Ten

Greg got out of the car and stood outside the mission. He glanced around, scanning the street for any sign of danger to Angelica. Still in the backseat, she looked small and delicate. Fragile. Until today he'd only seen strength. Every time he thought about what that brick could have done to her, his heart began to pound painfully in his chest. He could have lost her.

He bent down to pluck her from the car. "Come on. Let's get you on up to your apartment and settled. You look exhausted," he told her.

"Greg, you don't have to carry me," Angelica protested, her emerald-green eyes shy and disconcerted, even as her arms curled naturally around his neck. "Everyone will think I was badly hurt, or that there's something going on between us."

He frowned and glanced at Manny, who grinned and mouthed, "Good luck." Then said aloud, "I'll hold the door."

Greg almost told her that there *was* something between them, and that she was blind if she couldn't see it. But he wasn't sure how she felt about it. She might be appalled by the attraction between them, considering what she thought she knew about him. She'd only shown him friendship, after all. He might be the only one who wanted more. So, instead of blurting out his dreams of a future for them, he shifted her more securely in his arms and started for the steps.

"You were badly hurt. A concussion's nothing to fool with. Brian wanted to keep you in there overnight. Remember?"

"But he did release me," she argued.

"Only because I promised to take care of you. And I intend to do just that. Starting with putting you where you belong. In your bed."

"Why do I get the feeling that I'm going to pay for every minute I made you rest after that fight with Sam Jackson?"

Greg chuckled as he shouldered his way into the mission. "Can't imagine."

"Humph! I'll just bet you can't."

Most of the residents waited in the main room, anxious to see their angel. Angelica looked pale and weary, and they were visibly shaken to see her so low. The proverbial pin dropping would have sounded like a clanging cymbal in the room they'd entered. Remembering the torture he'd gone through, waiting to hear how she was, Greg set her down in a chair and gave them a quick rundown of her injuries. He warned them all of her need for several days' rest.

"He said one or two days," Angelica contradicted.

"He said he *preferred* that it was more. So it'll be more," he ordered. Angelica blinked in surprise at his tone, but he didn't give her the opportunity to challenge him. He scooped her into his arms again. "And now it's time to get you tucked in. Jean Ann, could you come along and help Miss Angelica get undressed?"

Only too happy to help, Jean Ann lumbered along behind them.

"Who made you boss?" Angelica grumbled, but it was a weak protest.

Greg grinned. "My brother. Your doctor." He had her there. In effect, she'd been released into his custody.

"Obviously a conspiracy," she retorted, sounding petulant and utterly adorable as she attempted to pout. But her out-of-character display didn't last long. Her inquiring mind soon moved on to a stickier subject.

"Greg, if you have family nearby, why were you homeless when you came here?"

It was the perfect opportunity for him to take Jim's advice, but all Greg could think, as he walked up the stairs holding her, was that the truth could do what the brick had not. Make him lose her. And hot on the heels of holding her in his arms, Greg just couldn't bring himself to chance it. "I'm trying to work through some problems," he told her instead. "My family has nothing to do with them, so I haven't wanted to burden them."

"From what your brother said, it sounds as if you've worried them anyway, and as if your problems have a root in your family."

"That's my brother's imagination. He doesn't understand."

"I know how not being understood by family feels,

Greg, but your parents at least seem to care for you. Promise me you'll go down to my office and call them. It sounds as if your father isn't well.''

Greg nodded. ''All right. I'll call after you're settled.''

A half hour later Greg returned to her room with a tray in his hands and several VCR tapes under his arm. ''Some of the neighborhood women cooked dinner, while Manny was waiting at the hospital,'' he said, setting the tray on her lap. ''I didn't want you to miss this. Chicken and dumplings. Do you feel up to eating a little?''

Angelica moved gingerly, wincing at the pain. ''Not really.''

''Try, okay? You need the nourishment.''

''Hmm. Where have I heard that one before?'' she asked.

Greg laughed quietly. ''Okay, so I was a lousy patient,'' he said ruefully. ''The question here is, are you going to act completely out of character to pay me back, or are you going to accept your situation gracefully and do what you know is right?''

She sighed. ''I'll be good. What else have you got there?''

''Some VCR tapes from the entertainment room— circa fifties. A cowboy flick and a seafaring tale,'' he told her, giving the titles of the classics. ''You game?''

''Sure, but my television's in the living room. I'll just get up and join you there.''

''No, you won't. I'll move the stuff in here.''

Greg quickly moved the television and the VCR into the bedroom and settled into a chair next to her bed. But the conversation he'd had with his mother swirled through his head, blocking out the decades-old dialogue coming from the TV set. Her advice was the same as Jim's: tell Angelica his identity as soon as possible. But she looked so small and pale lying there, her eyes dazed with pain and fatigue. And later, he was afraid the truth would destroy any chance he had with her.

He glanced next to him, noticing that Angelica's eyelids were closing. She looked like a child, fighting sleep until the last. What he did next wasn't something he thought about. Certainly nothing he planned. Greg found himself leaning forward, and drawn by an ache in his heart the size of the state and a moment's overwhelming tenderness, he touched his lips to hers.

He knew how a novice skydiver must feel a moment after stepping out of a perfectly good plane—desperately wanting to take back the rash step, yet unable to deny the sheer exhilaration of it all. Because for Greg there was no turning back, either, and he was desperately afraid that his fall would end with pain. But there was no ignoring the sharp spiral of desire that shot through his body.

He pulled his lips from hers and sat back in the chair. His breath dammed in his throat when he looked into her luminous green eyes. He hoped what he saw shining there was the same sudden awakening that he'd experienced, but he wasn't brave enough at that moment to ask.

"Try to sleep, Angel," he told her, hardly recognizing his own rough voice. "I'll be right here."

"Why do you call me Angel?" she asked, her voice shaky.

Greg smiled. "Because you are—" he watched her eyes drift shut as she fell instantly into a deep healing sleep, and he finished the thought aloud "—my angel."

He sat staring at the figures on the screen, hearing and seeing none of the movie. He wanted to get up and pace. To do something! Anything!

So this is love, he thought.

He had the good grace to laugh silently at himself. He'd had his share of relationships—teenage crushes and more serious adult attachments. But in his heart he knew he'd always remained curiously unmoved, untouched. No woman had ever swept him away on this tidal wave of emotion. Not even Jessie. Jessie had been a strikingly beautiful woman and he'd loved her, but now he could see that the love he'd felt for her was that for a friend, a trusted companion. It paled in comparison to his feelings for Angelica. He'd often thought there was something missing in him. He didn't think so anymore.

He glanced at Angel and felt a renewal of the longing that had pierced him earlier. What he felt for her was anything but friendly. And it was bound to be a problem in an already complicated assignment.

Angelica lay in bed the next afternoon, remembering the day before. Mostly she thought about Greg's good-night kiss and the feelings it had kindled in her. She'd dated when she'd had time, though not since her life had become filled with her work at the mission. But no one's kiss had ever felt the way Greg's

had. It had been a sweet, tender kiss, lasting only
seconds, but it had rocked her world and redefined
her idea of male-female relationships.

And it had settled once and for all the question of
why she was attracted to Greg. Suddenly it was clear.
Her feelings for him were not a rebellious attraction
spurred by her animosity toward her parents and their
values. She didn't believe in chance. What she did
believe was that God had a plan for each of his children, which meant Greg's arrival at the mission had
been part of His plan for each of them.

Greg had awakened her several times during the
night, concern written on his features. But there had
been something electric and edgy in his clear blue
eyes, as well. They'd shone like lightning and were
twice as vibrant.

He was gone now. Yet another pipe in need of his
attention had dragged him from her bedside. She
smiled. He'd certainly gone reluctantly. He'd even
taken a few extra minutes to wrest a solemn promise
of good behavior from her, while Emanuel shouted
about the water that was spraying all over his kitchen.

Of course, being on her good behavior today was
easy. Her head felt like a drum-and-bugle corps was
marching and playing inside it. The stitched cuts
throbbed, tugging painfully with every movement she
made. But though she wasn't up to doing anything
but lying in bed, she was bored and restless.

"Mail call!" Greg said, poking his head in the
doorway of her bedroom.

Angelica's heart sped up at the sight of him, but
she managed to sound composed. "Oh, good. I can
certainly handle paperwork from here."

Greg glared. "No, you can't. And it's not that kind of mail. This is especially for you." He dropped a stack of children's artwork in her lap.

"Get well cards?"

"Get well drawings, anyway," Greg qualified.

Angelica's throat ached as tears filled her eyes in spite of the witless smile she felt blooming on her face. "The day care kids made them. Oh. They're wonderful."

"Wait till you see the one Gina made. I look like a cross between a space man and a grizzly bear." His smile was so tender that her heart ached. "But you look like the angel from the top of a Christmas tree."

She wished that it didn't hurt to laugh when she got to the one he'd described. "Goodness, you do have a rather large head. But I really think she has the hair pretty nearly perfect."

"Ah, now come on. I never looked that bad. Did I?"

Angelica let out an unladylike snort. "You should have seen what you looked like by the time I woke up in the emergency room."

Greg sat at the bottom of the bed and leaned back against the footboard with his arms crossed over his chest, pretending to sulk. "Humph. Next time I do a running tackle and roll across the floor as glass rains down on me, I'll stop to comb my hair before I rush the ingrate to the hospital."

Angelica laughed. "The ingrate thanks you for taking such good care of her, but she's bored out of her gourd. My head hurts too much to read, and daytime TV is abominable. What am I supposed to do all day?"

"We could play a board game," he suggested. "Do you like chess?"

Greg's eyes sparkled. "Chess? Prepare to be vanquished."

In the alcove on the third floor corridor, Greg leaned back against the wall, folded his arms, and crossed one ankle over the other. He grinned, anticipating the look on Angelica's face when she came around the corner from her apartment. Gina's mother, Carmen, had sent Gina to fetch him. Apparently Angel was about to make a break for freedom on day two of her convalescence.

He'd spent a lot of time thinking about her since that kiss the other night. That wonderful kiss that had been the single worst mistake of his life. Not because of what it had told him about himself and his feelings for Angel, but because it had complicated an already hopelessly tangled situation.

Angel's reaction was unmistakable. She cared for him more than just a friend. Now when she heard the truth, she'd be even more hurt than if he had kept his feelings completely hidden. She might even think that he'd been using her and her feelings to further his case. It wasn't true, but Greg doubted the truth would help at this late date.

So he'd decided to hide any feelings he had for her that were not within the strict bounds of friendship. And in a few days when she was stronger, he'd tell her the truth. But in the meantime, he intended to make sure she rested—even if he had to lock her in her room.

Greg narrowed his eyes, listening, and couldn't

fight his growing grin as the footsteps pattered toward him. Footsteps that clearly were being made by someone sneaking along the hall.

"Hi there, Miss Angelica," he whispered as she passed him. "Where are we sneaking off to on this fine summer day?"

She froze in her tracks and pivoted slowly toward him. Greg burst out laughing at her aggrieved expression. "You were spying on me!" she said.

For a change those words didn't fill him with guilt, because this time his spying had been for her own good. "Yep," he said happily. "And quite a success I was. Imagine finding you up and about. On your way to your office, I hear."

"Who told you that? Maybe I was just stretching my legs."

"A little bird told me. And since I can't see any reason for you to get all dressed up just to venture out into the hall, I'd guess the little bird told it straight."

Angelica looked down at the skirt of her dress and held it out as if for inspection. "This old thing? This isn't dressed up."

"You look wonderful no matter how old it is. But then you always do," he heard himself say. He could have bitten his tongue when he saw her pleased smile. Why did his good intentions always fly out the nearest exit whenever she was near? His comment even had been off the subject he wanted to pursue.

"Thank you," she said, and smiled broadly.

"And I'd thank *you* if you'd turn around and go back to bed. Are you trying to get me in more trouble with my little brother? I promised him that I'd take care of you. I wouldn't be doing it real well if I let you go back to work too soon.''

''Oh, come on. How tired could I get just looking through the mail and making a few calls?''

With difficulty, Greg adopted a stern expression. She reminded him of a child trying to avoid bedtime. ''Getting tired at all is against doctor's orders. He said 'rest.' Now, march,'' he told her, pointing back down the hall to her apartment.

Angelica let out a groan. ''All right. But just for the rest of today. And you have to come give me a chance to redeem myself. Nobody ever trounced me at chess the way you did. Maybe I'd have better luck at Chinese Checkers.''

''I really should get to—''

''Hey, I'm bored. Either you come play, or I go to work. I promise not to tell that dragon lady you work for.''

Greg felt the blood drain from his face. Did she know he'd called her that to cover his true feelings when dealing with pushers? Something of what the phrase did to him must have shown on his face.

She reached out, laid her hand on his arm and gently squeezed. ''Greg, relax. I know the less desirable elements in the neighborhood call me that and worse. It's okay. If I wasn't getting to their consciences, they wouldn't give me a second thought. Now, come on.'' She turned and walked toward her apartment, calling over her shoulder, ''I get the red marbles.''

Greg followed. Reluctance and anticipation warred in his heart. He knew he should stay away from her. He was only getting in deeper with every moment they shared. Yet he needed to be with her the way he needed air to breathe. One of her smiles could make his day...and keep him awake at night.

Promising himself that he'd keep their time strictly within the bounds of friendship, Greg sat on the floor by the mahogany coffee table and moved a few things to make room for the checkerboard. She would sit on the sofa, he decided. The table would be safely between them. It would just be a game between friends, he assured himself. He was only there to cheer her, to relieve her boredom and restlessness. That was all this was—all it could be.

Angelica returned from her hall closet with the star-shaped game board and a box of marbles. She halted in the doorway, arrested by the sight of Greg sitting on her living room floor. And by the faraway look in his azure eyes as he stared into space. His expression was unreadable, but almost painfully beautiful in the light of a nearby window.

She loved him.

There was no way to deny that what she felt for him was more than friendship or even attraction. Too long hair, shaggy beard and all, she loved this gentle, social misfit with a heart of gold, solid principles and a mind-numbing, thousand-watt grin.

She just plain loved him.

"I guess I should have asked before we decided on a game," she said, and sat down on the floor next to him. She wanted to be near him, not separated by nearly a yard of mahogany.

Greg blinked back to the moment, clearly surprised that she'd settled so close beside him. "Asked?" His voice came out as a croak. He swallowed deeply and scooted about a foot farther away. "Asked what?"

Angelica eyed him with an eyebrow raised in mock suspicion. "Just how often have you played Chinese Checkers?" she asked, fighting not to show the hurt that his retreat had caused her. "After the way you dethroned me as Mission Chess Champ, I need to be more careful of the opponents I choose."

"You're probably safe. I haven't played in years. But I used to play a lot as a kid."

Sadness reflected in his eyes, even as what she was beginning to think of as a mask fell over his face. She could usually see something guarded in the stillness of his features that was only missing when he laughed. His eyes, however, always gave him away. It was suddenly vital to Angelica that she understand what that flash of sadness had meant. Maybe then she'd understand the facade and the secrets it guarded.

"Hmm. Not since you were a kid, huh?" she said thoughtfully, a teasing smile tipping her lips upward at the corners. "And just who did you play with? The Chinese Checker champ of the Orient?"

He grinned, and her heart and stomach did their usual flip-flop. "My brothers and my father," he told her. "Dad has a fishing cabin in the Poconos." Greg chuckled, his eyes crinkling at the corners. "Well, my mother—the one and only time she came with us— dubbed it The Shack." He shook his head after an eye-narrowing moment of thought. "That may have been a little too kind."

Angelica shuddered. "I can almost see the spiders. It sounds like my worst nightmare."

"Spiders were the least of the livestock. Yeah."

He sighed in deep satisfaction. "A real 'guy' kind of place, that's what it was. Dad used to take us there for the weekends a few times in the spring and summer. It was the only way he really got a weekend off. If customers called with problems, Dad just couldn't turn them down. He's retired now."

"You miss him. And your mother, don't you?"

His eyes took on an absent but thoughtful expression. "Yeah, but sometimes life just gets in the way. You know."

She knew. "So you played Chinese Checkers at the cabin?"

Greg nodded, then laughed. "At nights. The nights were the worst. Boring. No TV. No electricity, in fact. And we'd hear things scurrying around in the dark corners. Playing games kept us too busy to think about them when we were young, and they were a nightly tradition by the time we were in our teens.

"We loved going there with Dad. Lazy days in the wide open spaces. It was the life! And Dad didn't care how dirty we got—which is always a plus when you're a kid."

"So you filled the creepy nights with games?"

"Of any kind. We'd play till, one by one, we'd fall asleep and Dad would tuck us in. There was no set bedtime at the shack. Another plus when you're ten. Then one weekend he turned in before us."

"Is that when your weekends stopped?"

Greg shrugged. "We got too old." His voice was flat—the flash of pain back in his eyes again behind the careful mask.

"Was that about the time you lost your brother?" she asked, probing carefully.

Now there was something akin to panic peeking out from behind the camouflage. "You heard Brian in the ER," he said, his tone as carefully neutral as the expression he valiantly tried to maintain.

Drawn by the poignancy of his struggle, Angelica reached out to lay her hand on his shoulder. "I woke up and I could hear, but I couldn't open my eyes. I could hear the pain in Brian's voice and yours. Please don't think I was eavesdropping on purpose."

He put his hand over hers and gently squeezed. "Of course you weren't. And, yeah, that was the year the weekends stopped. We didn't go anymore after Tommy…died. Everything was different after that."

"Was he older or younger than you?"

"Younger. How about you? Who'd you play checkers with?" His voice was falsely bright and didn't fool Angelica for a second. She recognized his blatant attempt to get the focus off himself, as well, but she could also see that he'd grown tense.

"My Gran," she said, yielding to his silent entreaty. "Checkers, Chess, Cribbage. She loved games that made you think. That's probably why she never got old. She stayed young till the day she died in her eighties."

"You were close?"

Angelica knew her smile was wistful as she crossed two fingers and held them up. "We were like that. I spent nearly every holiday and summer with her when I was young. Then I moved in with her after I graduated from college. She taught me to follow my dreams. Even when it turned out that my dreams were destined to bring me here, she encouraged me."

"What *are* your dreams? You tell everyone here

that they can achieve their fondest wishes but—what about yours?''

''What do I want? I want the mission to bear fruit in this community. I want a family someday. I want to always serve the Lord, no matter what I'm doing. How about you?''

He stared into her eyes and touched her cheek. She thought—she hoped—he'd kiss her again. But he suddenly pulled his hand back as if touching her had burned him. ''I—I can't. Not yet,'' he whispered, his voice hoarse. Then he scooted another foot away. ''Let's get to our rematch! Got any green marbles?''

Chapter Eleven

"I'm supposed to be your boss, remember?" Angelica complained to Greg after dinner several nights later. The fact that he didn't even blink at the annoyance and sarcasm in her tone, tried her already stretched patience even more. How much rest and placating could one person stand!

"Nicest one I've ever had," he said.

His smile was so sweet that she wanted to scream. "So how come I feel as if I should be thanking you for letting me come down for tonight's services?"

"I never said you need to thank me," he said. "But I guess you could thank Judge Whiting for finally coming for services tonight."

"You know what I mean. I feel like a prisoner about to be released," she grumbled.

Greg walked back to the small conversation area and sat opposite her. "Angel, I'm sorry you're climbing the walls. And I'm sorry you've felt so trapped by needing to rest. But please, don't go so wild with your freedom that you try to do more than greet the judge and enjoy the service. That dizzy spell you had Wednesday night scared me half to death.''

How was she supposed to stay annoyed at someone who was being so nice? "You worry too much. Brian said it wasn't all that unusual.''

Greg shook his head. "He also extended your rest for several days. If I hadn't called to get him to okay tonight, you'd still be in bed—where you probably belong.''

Angelica sat back against the sofa cushions and crossed her arms. She knew she'd needed the rest to help her heal, but she wasn't ready to admit it to her jailer. "So nice of you to take pity on me,'' she groused.

Greg's smile never faltered. He was clearly unperturbed by her ill-humor. "It isn't pity. It's worry. We all want you back, but only when you're ready. Tomorrow will come soon enough. Tonight, you just sit back and take joy from the service, okay?''

"The band! I usually lead the singing, and we haven't even practiced this week. And I never confirmed with Pastor Joe. How could I forget?''

"You were hurt. So I handled it all. Brian said you shouldn't be subjected to the stress of standing up in front of a crowd and singing.''

"It isn't stress. It's praising the Lord. I like to sing.''

He shook his head again and stood. "Brian said 'no.' But don't worry. The gym's all set up, and the band's tuning up. I found someone else to lead the worship, and they got together to practice last night. It'll all be fine. Now I have to go—ah…check with the band. Why don't you just relax for a few more minutes, then come on down?"

"Rest," she grumbled. "Relax," she added, as he opened her front door. "Brian said," she mimicked in a deep voice. "You're enjoying watching me climb the walls!" she shouted at him as he closed the door behind him.

Then the final indignity: Greg's burst of laughter echoing back at her from down the hall.

Ten minutes later, Angelica approached Harold and Estelle Whiting as they entered the big main room of the mission. "Welcome. I'm so glad you could come."

"It was so kind of you to invite us, dear," Estelle said, clasping Angelica's hand. "We were so distressed to hear of your injuries. How are you feeling?"

"Much better. I'm anxious to get back to work tomorrow."

"You mustn't overdo," Harold Whiting said. "Concussions are nothing to fool with."

Angelica laughed. "You don't need to worry about me overdoing it. The health gestapo is in full force around here. They'll probably make me take a nap with the day care kids for a week. Greg Peters even has the children spying on me to make sure I behave. You have no idea how grateful I am that you decided to come tonight. You gained me an early reprieve." Angelica smiled and glanced at the clock on the wall. "Why don't we go inside? The service should be starting soon."

Minutes later she slid into the first row next to Agnes, who'd come in behind her husband. Angelica said a quick prayer for the Lord's blessing on her efforts with the judge. This was the opportunity she'd been waiting for with him. He saw faith as a duty to obey a series of man-made laws governing religious behavior. It was a joyless existence, and because of it he was as rigid as the Pharisees must once have been.

Like so many people, he didn't understand the freedom and peace granted through a personal relationship with Jesus, or the joy brought by following the Lord's wishes for his life.

That was one of the things she'd tried to show her parents, but she'd failed. Angelica retreated from the stab of pain that thoughts of her parents always brought. She was instantly grateful that the band's leader had stepped to the microphone.

He welcomed guests and then welcomed a new singer and worship leader who he said had become a major part of the family of North Riverside Mission in just a few short weeks. Angelica's eyes flew open, stunned to see Greg stand and walk up the two steps of the platform. He perched on a stool and lifted a guitar onto his lap. He closed his eyes and offered a plainspoken prayer of praise. Then he stopped and looked toward Angelica, offering a prayer of thanks for her presence among them, and one of petition for her continued healing.

The sound of Greg's beautiful voice held everyone spellbound for the first several verses of a paraphrased Psalm 123, then one after another the voices of the congregation joined his, until they were all singing. While several more songs filled the air with praise, an offering basket passed informally through the worshipers.

Angelica felt a stab of disappointment when the basket came forward from the row behind, and Judge Whiting made a grand show of laying a fifty-dollar bill on top of the pile of change and dollar bills given from the hearts of those less fortunate. She forgot her momentary dismay that he'd missed what she'd been trying to show him, when Greg began to read from I Corinthians 13:4-8.

"What kind of love is Paul speaking of here?" Greg asked after the reading. "Have you ever looked at these words and at the world? At ourselves? Can anyone here say they've never been rude, been glad when someone they're not too crazy about has faced misfortune, never thought the worst of someone, never sought credit for a good work? I know I sure couldn't say that. It's not something I'm proud of, but I can't sit here and pretend to be perfect.

"Paul isn't writing this to make us feel badly about ourselves. He doesn't expect us to be perfect. He'd like us to strive to be as close to perfect as we can be, though. In Matthew 5:47, Jesus tells us, 'Be perfect even as your heavenly father is perfect.'

"So here in I Corinthians, if this love Paul's talking about is perfect love, whose love is he talking about? This has to be God's love. Christ's love. If you're not sure, try putting His name in place of the word love. Then try putting your own in there. You'll see. This is about Him. About the way He loves each one of us. *His* love bears all things. Jesus bears all things, believes all things, hopes all things, endures all things.

"His love never fails. *Jesus* never fails."

Angelica listened for the next half hour as Greg continued to tell the people how much God loved them and how it was their duty to love each other as much as they could. He showed them ways to love, depths of love, and promised that the more they tried to love others, the easier it would get—the happier they'd all be. It was as inspiring and uplifting, yet humbling, a message as she'd ever heard. Greg truly had a gift.

She wondered if he even knew.

Greg's solo of "Amazing Grace" and his own heartfelt closing prayer ended the service. Angelica had never enjoyed one more.

She excused herself from Judge and Mrs. Whiting and went to Greg, who stood chatting with the band and some of the mission residents at the front of the gym. "Why didn't you tell me you were the one doing tonight's service?"

"Pastor Joe was supposed to be here, but he was up sick all night. I was afraid you'd worry more if I told you that I was the only one I could find." He grimaced. "I was pretty nervous. It's been years since I used to lead youth worship at my church. And I know I'm not Whiting's favorite employee around here."

"And if he says anything, I'll tell him you're important to us—to me."

Greg frowned a bit as if bothered by her words, but then his gaze strayed from hers. "Well, it looks as if you'll get the opportunity. Here comes the judge," he quipped in a perfect imitation of the old vaudeville line.

It was typical of Greg to hide uncertainty with humor. That Whiting's reaction mattered so much to him warmed her heart because she knew his only concern was how the judge's opinion would affect her. But it also added to her worry over how enigmatic he'd been ever since he'd kissed her. What was going on in his mind?

When he'd first come to the mission, Greg had been embarrassed by his appearance and had looked wounded when she'd alluded to it. It had bothered her before that she might have let her upbringing prejudice her toward him in some way. She had dismissed the thought then, but now had to wonder again if she'd led him to believe that she found him to be unworthy of her. Was he embarrassed by that heart-awakening kiss they'd shared because of some unconscious signal she'd given him?

Pondering that worry, she turned toward her approaching guests. "Judge Harold Whiting and Mrs. Whiting, this is Greg Peters."

"Pleased to meet you, Your Honor, ma'am," Greg said, and offered his hand to the judge.

The judge shook his hand and said, "Good to meet you, son. You have a very impressive voice. From your appearance, I would expect you to lean more toward rock and roll than church music. Of course, except for "Amazing Grace," the rest of what you and that band did sounded more like rock than anything I've ever heard at a religious service."

"The Bible tells us to make a joyful noise unto the Lord, Harold. He doesn't tell us what beat or instruments to use," Angelica put in.

Estelle Whiting stepped forward and put her hand

on Angelica's arm. "You're so right, dear. You mustn't pay Harold any mind at all. He just hates change. Your insights into Corinthians were thought-provoking, Greg. I enjoyed your teaching. It seemed more like teaching than a sermon—an interesting idea for a service. Yes, I liked it a lot. It's so much harder to ignore something you've actually learned than something you've only been told."

"Thank you," Greg said.

"I'm so proud of you. It was a wonderful message," Angelica told him, hoping he'd believe her. She looked up into his deep blue eyes and lost her train of thought.

Judge Whiting cleared his throat. "Didn't I hear something about dessert in the dining hall?"

It was nearly ten the next morning when Greg heard a human bellow that sounded more like a roar resound up the basement steps. He and Angelica met at the top of the cellar stairs. Greg frowned down at her. "You stay here. I'll see what Manny's problem is. It's my job."

"Far be it from me to keep a man from his work. And from the sound of Emanuel's bellow, I'd say it's a problem of catastrophic proportions. By all means," she said, gesturing him forward with a mockingly dramatic sweep of her hand. She laughed when he scowled at her as he passed. He loved her laugh. It was rich and captivatingly joyful.

Thinking more of Angel than Manny's emergency, Greg stepped off the bottom step and into two inches of water. It appeared that the order of the day had changed from plaster to plumbing. He shot a disgusted look at Manny, who'd sounded the alarm. "You could have warned me."

Manny snickered and looked past him up the steps toward Angel. "If you had your mind on the problem, man, and not the angel, you'd have been looking where your feet were going."

Greg's ears picked up the sound of still-running water. "Well, I'm thinking about water now. Why didn't you turn it off?"

Manny shrugged. "I tried, but the valve isn't working. Turning it off didn't even slow the water down."

"The valve to what?" Greg asked, though dreading the answer.

"To the hot water heater. I didn't have any when I started on the breakfast dishes. I came down to see what was up."

"The tide, huh?" Greg sighed. It looked like his day was planned. His father would love to see this. *Plumbing.* Greg really hated plumbing.

He waded over to the burst hot water heater. The valve was obviously worn out. "Terrific. I'll have to turn it off at the main. And that means no water in any part of the building until I can at least get a new valve in."

"So, what's the plan?" Manny asked.

Greg put the new valve on the counter at Murphy's Hardware store and reached in his back pocket for the cash Angelica had given him. He'd rushed upstairs and explained the emergency, so Angel had given him a fifty-dollar bill and sent him to the local hardware store. The valve would cost a buck more than at the big plumbing supplier that was halfway across the city. He'd sent Manny there for the hot water heater, but the mission's facilities would be back on line in less than an hour this way.

Mr. Murphy came out of the back room and smiled. "Son, you're getting to be a real regular around here."

Greg smiled back at the older man and pulled the money Angel had given him out of his back pocket. "It seems as if the Lord held back the flood of repairs Angelica needed to have done till someone came along who could do them," he replied.

"Flood would seem to be the apt word, young fellow." Murphy laughed and tapped the counter with the valve.

Greg tossed the fifty down next to the valve under Murphy's hand. And his heartrate doubled. He picked the bill back up and stared at it. It was marked. His mark. There was no mistaking it. Had there been a bill in his pocket already from one of the nights when he'd made a buy?

"Something wrong with that bill, son?" Murphy asked.

Greg looked back at Murphy. " It—isn't the one I was supposed to spend. Hold on a minute?"

Greg stuffed his hands into his front pockets and came up empty. The only other money he had was in his wallet. So the bill had to have come from Angel. It couldn't mean the obvious. He wouldn't believe she had anything to do with the people he'd bought the drugs from.

He couldn't spend it, so he pulled out his wallet and paid with his own money. Folding the fifty in fours to keep it separate, he tucked it into the ID pocket of his wallet. But he couldn't put the worry away as easily.

Four hours later he'd hooked up the new water heater and the bill still sat in his wallet, his conscience burning. Never in his career had he withheld any kind of evidence during an ongoing investigation. And he knew he couldn't do it now. He'd racked his brain while doing the job, trying to figure out how Angelica could have gotten that bill. The Sunday night collection was the only innocent way he'd come up with. Unfortunately, he'd identified everyone at the Sunday service, and they all appeared as innocent as Angelica. And she was the only one who'd ever been a suspect in the case. If he reported this, he was afraid she would become one again.

And by the next morning that was exactly what had happened. Under orders, Greg had the bugs back in operation; Angelica was a suspect again, though he'd staunchly defended her. Worse, his window of opportunity to tell her the truth about himself had closed. What should have been a ray of hope—the phony raid as part of the sting operation was set for the next day, which meant the end of the assignment was nearer—didn't even brighten his dark mood. All the end of the assignment meant was that Angel would soon learn of his lies, and she'd be out of his life forever.

Angelica stared at the object in her hand. "What on earth is it?" she wondered aloud. It looked like a watch battery, but it was too big to fit in any watch she'd ever seen. She glanced at the doorway in response to a knock. She smiled. Greg always seemed to show up whenever she needed him. Even if it was just to talk.

"Greg, have you got any idea what this is? I found it on the floor just inside the conference room."

Greg frowned and walked in. He took it from her, staring at it for a few moments, then he shrugged carelessly. "It's sticky on one side. Maybe it's part of a fancy button that fell apart. You know the kind on women's dresses and suits." He stuck it in his shirt pocket. "One of the women you counsel could have lost it in here. I'll stick it in the lost-and-found box."

Ever helpful Greg. "I could have walked to the front desk, you know."

"Hey, no problem. I'm headed that way, anyhow. I just wanted to tell you that I'm going over to help Manny get his sister's new refrigerator up to her apartment. Oh, and Jean Ann's at the front desk. She said to tell you that your next appointment's here. The woman just took her kids up to Kids' Corner, and she'll be down as soon as they're settled."

"Thanks. I'll get back to the conference room then. Will you be back by dinner?"

"Yeah. I should be."

"Oh, good. You've been so busy helping neighbors in your off-hours that I've hardly seen you in a week."

"Yeah. Well, like you said, I've been busy. See ya, then."

Angelica stared at Greg's retreating back. She wished he'd never kissed her, because ever since then he'd been... It was hard to describe. "Aloof" was wrong. He was too friendly to ever be called stand-offish. "Wary" came to mind. Yes, that was it. That was an apt description of what she saw in his eyes whenever he looked at her now.

She had let him know that she valued him and saw him as a worthwhile person. So maybe the problem was that even if he'd come to care for her, it was still too soon after his loss of Jessie. She could certainly understand that he would feel loyal to a woman he'd obviously loved and had lost in such a tragic way.

Angelica was determined to give him all the time he needed. She wouldn't rush him or push him. She would just love him from a distance if that was what he needed. She would love him and pray for him until he was ready to face what it was that had bloomed between them.

Greg stepped into an alley and pulled out his cell phone. He got his friend's voice mail. "Jim. Greg. What did they do, cut the budget on glue? It didn't even hold for a week! You know by now what she found in the conference room. I'm checking the rest of them tonight, and if they're at all loose, I'm pulling them!"

"Hey man, you tryin' to call me?"

Greg stiffened at the sound of the voice behind him, then relaxed. The kid was far enough away that he couldn't have heard what was said. Greg hit the "off" button on his cell phone, and turned. It was one of the pushers he'd dealt with in the past.

"No. I was calling a friend, trying to borrow money. I'm a little short right now."

"I could make arrangements."

"Thanks, but I thought I'd give quitting another try," Greg told him.

"Hey, don't worry about the money. Here." He held out a bag of white powder. "No sense suffering. You want it. You know you do."

Greg reached out to take it, making his hand shake. Then he pulled back and shook his head.

"I need to quit."

"Then take it just in case you can't do without. Maybe use it sort of as a crutch. Like if you know it's there, you might not need it so much. Look at your hands shake, man. You know you need it bad."

If he didn't take it, someone else would wind up with it, Greg realized. He held out his hand, knowing that an addict would probably cave in about then, anyway. He knew, too, that this was a pusher's trick to keep a customer addicted. Greg wanted this guy in the worst way. "Okay. Just this once. But I'm not gonna use it. How come you're being so…you know—generous?"

"'Cause if you decide not to go straight, you'll come to me. I like having steady customers." He laughed, gesturing to Greg's shaking hand. "And not-so-steady ones, too. See you around."

Greg watched the kid weave his way around the trash in the alley, and exit at the opposite end from where he'd entered. Greg turned and started out of the alley.

A patrol car pulled to a stop in front of him, just as Greg pocketed the drugs. And he knew. They'd seen the product. His cover was either blown, or he'd be spending the night in lockup. Either way, Angel was about to find out the truth, or fire him for drug use. And either way, she'd hate him.

"You must know the drill. Hands on the back of your head."

Greg complied, wondering how these two would feel when they found out what side of the badge he'd been on when he'd learned "the drill."

One patrolman—Hunter, his tag said—fished the bag out of Greg's shirt pocket while the other cuffed him.

"I thought you worked over at the mission," Hunter said.

"I do," Greg said. "It was just lying in the alley. I couldn't leave it there for some kid to pick up. I was going to flush it. Really." Even to his own ears the story sounded unbelievable. He probably wouldn't have swallowed it, but these cops were with the Third. There was still hope.

"Sure. Tell it to the Judge," Hunter said.

Greg's stomach turned over. And then again, maybe this would be a problem, after all. "The Judge?" he asked.

"Judge Whiting. And don't get your hopes up. We don't screw up our evidence," the other one, Officer DeVega, said. "You have the right to remain..."

Just my luck, Greg thought—not even listening to the words he'd spoken so often himself. He'd stumbled on probably the only two honest cops working out of the Third.

Twelve hours later Greg's was the first arraignment of the morning. He stood in confused, stunned silence. Nothing was going the way he'd thought it would. It was going better. Too much better. It made no sense.

"You say you didn't see him buy the drugs, so the defendant, who is a true asset to this community, could be telling the truth?" Whiting asked Hunter.

Hunter chuckled. "Well, anything's possible, but you ought to hear some of the stories we hear. It was still in his possession, after all."

Whiting's expression darkened. He clearly saw no humor in Greg's stupid excuse, or in Hunter's amusement with it. "Did you inform Mr. Peters of his rights before or after he told you his intent toward the drugs?"

Hunter frowned. "After. But his statement hasn't got anything to do with his rights."

Hunter was right, and Greg could hardly believe his ears. He'd thought Whiting would throw the book at him. That he'd have to blow his cover with at least the judge. Now the man who'd once been ready to hang him out to dry for talking to a pusher was twisting a perfectly good arrest around to sound as if the officers had violated his rights.

"Actually, by giving a statement as to his intent with the drugs," Whiting continued, "the defendant admitted the drugs were in his possession. Therefore, he was admitting his guilt before his rights were read." The gavel slammed down. "Case dismissed. Next case, bailiff."

Greg felt the cuffs unsnapped from his wrists. He turned to his court-appointed attorney—an attorney who'd yet to say a word. Greg wondered who looked more shocked. Him, the young attorney, or DeVega, the officer who'd just uncuffed him. Greg longed to say something to both officers. To tell them they'd been right.

"I don't understand," he said to DeVega. "I was telling the truth but—"

"Just get out of here. There's nothing that makes me sicker than a hypocrite," Hunter said behind Greg.

Greg turned to Hunter and noticed that he was staring at Judge Whiting.

Judge Whiting? What was going on? Was the judge in league with the Third and the Judges? No, it couldn't be. Yet Greg felt that icy fist of certainty in the pit of his stomach that told him when an out-of-the-blue hunch was right on target.

It was the only thing that made sense. A man like Whiting wouldn't have let him off the hook just to protect the mission. The judge had struck him as the type to gloat because he'd been right and Angel had been wrong about Greg.

And he had the perfect cover. They all did. With a judge on the district bench, they operated in complete protection. Nothing had been able to touch them. Until Angelica had come to the neighborhood and had begun asking questions and wanting help from the governor's task force. Except she'd asked Judge Whiting for help first. No wonder they wanted her out of the way. With her gone, they'd have been unstoppable.

Greg followed the officers out of the courtroom in a semi-fog of racing thoughts and dazed emotions. The scope of the conspiracy was so big that it overwhelmed him.

"Why did he let me go?" Greg asked Hunter, playing dumb, hoping for some insight into the judge's actions from what appeared to be two honest officers.

"I mean, even if he believed me, that wasn't right, was it?"

The attorney spoke up. "It's one I'm going back to my office and look up, let me tell you." He walked away without further comment.

"Follow us. We'll get your property back," Hunter said. "Just don't talk to me. I just had my breakfast."

Greg felt like pond scum, but he couldn't explain. And he couldn't wait until he could. He'd be sure to let Internal Affairs know that these two officers were apparently clean. He was heartily sick of the whole assignment and the dirt he'd uncovered. He'd given up six years of his life to stop the flow of drugs into the city, and this bunch of opportunists, who'd sworn to uphold the law, had been using it with impunity.

It took longer than necessary for the return of his property, but Greg couldn't blame Hunter and De-Vega for their delaying tactics. They'd been furious—and with good reason. If it made facing their day a little easier to harass him, he didn't mind.

So it wasn't until two hours later that Greg approached the mission. He didn't know what to say to Angel. He didn't know if she had any idea where or how he'd spent the night. Had Whiting called her? If court was still in session, it was possible the judge hadn't had time. Should Greg try to give her the same story he'd given Hunter and DeVega?

He just couldn't seem to *think!* It felt like his brain was paralyzed. Numb.

Chapter Twelve

~❧~

Angelica watched Greg trudge slowly up the front steps as if his shoes were lined with lead. Her heart ached for him. He looked so tired and defeated. She still couldn't believe that those two policeman hadn't listened to him, or that they'd kept him in lockup all night. Greg was no more a drug user than she was. And she'd told the officers so, when they'd stopped to warn her about him. If he said that he picked up those drugs so he could destroy them, then that's what he'd done!

The look in Greg's eyes when she met him at the door nearly broke her. It was as if some vital part of him had been deeply injured. She rushed to him, hoping to reassure him that she didn't doubt his innocence. "It's all right. I know what happened. You go get some sleep. You look exhausted. We'll talk later."

Greg's eyes widened in surprise. "You don't want me to pack up and get out?"

Angelica frowned. "You wouldn't do what they said, Greg. Maybe you need to talk more than you need sleep. Why don't you tell me what happened? The truth."

"The truth?"

"The truth. What actually happened, and not what officers DeVega and Hunter *say* happened. I know you were planning to dispose of that heroin—not use it."

"Is that what it was? Heroin? I didn't know for sure, except that I didn't want it on the street," Greg agreed.

"So why would I ask you to leave? This was some sort of harassment on the part of the police. Thankfully, Judge Whiting was there to protect your rights."

"He didn't tell you to fire me again, I take it," Greg said, his tone as flat as the look in his eyes.

"No. He didn't tell me anything. I told him you'd been arrested. I called him last night after the two officers left here. He understood how you might do what you did. It might have been foolish, but we both understood why you would pick up a bag you were sure contained drugs to throw them out. Goodness, a child could have gotten hold of them. I'm so glad the judge talked them into dropping the charges."

Greg's eyes narrowed. "They didn't drop the charges. Judge Whiting threw the case out on a...a technicality."

She smiled. "I knew he'd help somehow. That's why I called him."

"It seemed out of character for him."

"He believed in your innocence immediately."

"But still, he's so strongly against drugs. After all, he's the one who tried to get the governor's task force to come in here."

"For all the good his pleading did," Angelica added, still angry over the governor's apathy toward North Riverside.

"No, it didn't do much good, did it? I don't understand how the governor could ignore a request from a judge like Whiting," Greg said, his voice hollow and deeply saddened. Angelica had never seen him so closed in on himself.

She put a hand on his shoulder. "I think maybe you *do* need to get some sleep."

"I slept in lockup. Don't worry about me. I'm fine. I'd like to get out of the neighborhood today, though. Would you mind if I took my day off today instead of tomorrow?"

Wishing he'd turn to her for the comfort he obviously needed, but remembering her vow to give him room, she shrugged. "Not at all. I'm sure a change in scenery would do you a world of good."

His voice oddly detached, he said, "Yeah, a world of good. I'll be back by tomorrow. I may go see my parents. Maybe stay the night." She watched him turn and walk back out without another word. He stopped at the bottom of the steps and scanned the neighborhood, then the sky. Standing there, he looked numb, as if the night in jail had truly taken something vital from him.

Greg stood in front of the clouded mirror above the dresser in his room at the mission late the next night. Still holding the razor he'd used in a fit of anger to virtually destroy his disguise, he stared at a face he scarcely recognized. The past twenty-four hours had shaken his belief in the system beyond a point where he thought that he could continue to be connected with it.

First had come his arrest and the revelation about Judge Whiting. He and Jim had spent the rest of yesterday and today researching Whiting's financial records. Through a paper trail of real estate sales and dummy companies, they'd traced the dealings of a leading citizen from the Bench to the gutter.

Then had come his last meeting with Torres a couple of hours earlier....

"Sit down, Peterson, Lovell," Captain Torres had said before looking at Greg. "I want you back at the mission. All of what you've learned still doesn't prove Angelica DeVoe's innocence."

Greg had started to protest but Torres put up his hand like that of a traffic cop. "Hold on there. It's plain how you feel about her innocence *and* her. Which could be coloring your judgment. She and Whiting are pretty chummy. He's one of her contributors, after all. It does give us more than just reasonable doubt about the marked bill, though. Whiting could very well have passed it to her without her knowledge. And we have something else against our esteemed judge—and this really ought to brighten your day, Peterson—Adam Jones is awake and talking. The night he was shot he *was* trying to tell you that it was one of the Judges who shot him, but he was also trying to warn you that Judge Whiting was mentioned as having ordered that propane tank turned on. Jones heard one of the Judges tell another to report to Whiting that the gas hadn't ignited because Jones got wise to them, and that Jones wouldn't be in the way next time.''

"Kind of gives you a new angle on that gang's name, doesn't it?'' Jim Lovell growled. "The Judges.''

"You two have built a good case against Whiting,'' Torres continued, "but it still doesn't clear Angelica DeVoe. I agree that she is *probably* innocent, but we can't go on probabilities and gut feelings. There could have been a falling-out among thieves to warrant his trying to have her killed.

"After yesterday, you're out of the business of making buys. I've cleared it with your captain. Right now your job is either prove that DeVoe is guilty or keep her safe. The case should be wrapped up in under a week. We'll continue the surveillance from the van on the remaining bugs until arrests are made. And we still want you to keep your true identity under wraps.''

The conversation with Torres had prompted Greg's decision to make this his last undercover assignment. There had to be a better way to make a difference.

Putting down the razor, Greg tilted his head and considered the stranger in the mirror. He hadn't yet divulged his identity, but with his hair tied back and the beard gone, he felt and looked more like Greg Peterson. Whoever that was. He swallowed, his throat aching.

Just as the face in the mirror blurred behind a sheen of embarrassing tears, a noise outside his small window drew Greg's attention. Angel's delicate figure, illuminated by the playground lights, moved toward the side gate. Greg glanced at his watch. Where was she going by herself at nearly ten-thirty at night? What was she thinking? Why was she going anywhere and especially after dark? She'd promised she wouldn't go out alone.

He was on the move a moment later. When he reached the playground gate, Greg saw her turn left down the street behind the mission. The only place she could be going in that direction was the park.

John Paul Jones Park lay along the southern border of North Riverside and overlooked the river that separated North Riverside from Riverside proper. The work weekend had improved it in appearance, but not in safety. It was a dark, unlit urban green-space full of old trees, cracked walkways and the occasional park bench.

Not wanting to alert any gang members who might be around to Angel's presence, Greg didn't call out her name, but followed about a block behind her. After maintaining a safe distance until she entered the park, Greg picked up the pace. A breeze off the river made it cooler here, and the faint scent of waning honeysuckle drifted on the air. "Angel," he called quietly. "Wait up."

She stopped and turned toward him. "I didn't know you'd gotten back. Are you all right?"

"Actually, I was about to ask you the same thing. Have you lost your mind? Walking alone like this at night would be dangerous even if the Judges weren't after you."

Angel shook her head and walked to a bench near the water. "I just needed...some air."

Greg's radar screamed at the slight catch in her throat. He followed and stood, watching her closely, as she settled on the recently painted, cement-and-wood park bench. When he saw the way her hands lay on her lap in a tangle of clinched fingers, he knew she was once again battling heartache alone. Couldn't she tell that he wanted nothing on this earth more than to be there for her in good times and bad?

"Next time you need air, go up to the roof. It'd be a whole lot safer. You're lucky no one saw you," he growled, instead of revealing his heart's desire.

"I didn't think. Sorry. I didn't mean to upset you. I guess I'm not used to anyone worrying about me," Angelica told him, her tone heartbreakingly bleak.

They were a really depressing pair, Greg thought ruefully, as he dropped down beside her. How had they both gotten so far from joy in the Lord, while living lives aimed at helping their fellow man? "What's wrong, Angel?"

She didn't look at him, but sniffed quietly. The sound of her tears twisted Greg's heart. He reached out and took her hand, entwining their fingers, then resting their clasped hands on his thigh. "Talk to me. Please. Let me help. You can't always be the one patching up the rest of us."

"You've done more patching up for me than anyone since Gran died. I don't know what I would have done without you these last weeks.

"Today was just a bad day. We found drugs in Antonio's routine blood work. I had to ask him to leave. Twenty minutes later, Emanuel saw him with several of the Judges."

"Well, that fingers our inside man. I'm sorry, Angel. I was afraid someone living inside the mission was only there to cause trouble. It explains how they got inside to mess with the locks and turn on the propane canister. And he was in the hall when I came out of your office. He must have signaled whoever threw the brick."

"I tried to help him," she said, pain and disappointment evident in her voice. "It hurts that he lied to me. I hate lies."

Greg swallowed. But you're here to help, he told himself. You didn't want to hurt her. She'll understand. She has to!

Angelica interrupted his troubled thoughts. "And the other thing was—oh, I'm being a big baby about this." She still hadn't even glanced at him.

"About what?" he asked. When she didn't answer, he sat back to wait in silence. He'd sit there holding her hand all night, if need be.

She sighed a sigh that was full of exasperation. "You are the most stubborn man. It's my birthday! Okay? There. I told you. I spent my birthday alone in a sea of people who were all trying to make it a special day."

"And knowing you, I'll bet you pretended to have a high old time for their sakes."

Angel shrugged, staring straight ahead, her delicate profile highlighted by the moonlight. She was so beautiful that it took his breath away. He wanted nothing more at that moment than to stand and pull her into his arms and kiss the sadness off her pretty mouth. But she needed something else—something less physical and infinitely more important. She needed understanding.

"I feel like a spoiled brat who got wonderful gifts but still isn't satisfied," she admitted in a hoarse voice.

"You don't have a spoiled bone in your body. Do you miss your family? Is that it?" Greg asked, watching a bevy of conflicting emotions move across her shadowed face.

"You see how selfish I'm being? As if you don't miss your family, too!"

"I do, so I understand how you feel. Except not completely. I don't fully understand what keeps you and your family apart."

"Lies. It's always been lies."

"I thought it was that they disapprove of your living here."

"There are a lot of problems and have been for years, but the mission brought it all to a head."

"A pretty lady once told me that if I talked about what was bothering me, I'd feel better."

"And you didn't talk—if I remember correctly," she replied, smiling faintly.

He snapped the fingers of his free hand. "You see. And I still feel rotten most of the time. Take your own advice, Angel. Talk about it," he urged.

Angelica nodded and bit her lip. After a few minutes of deep thought, she said, "I was almost finished with my master's in social science when I heard about how bad life was here on the North side. I was living with Gran and I talked about wanting to minister to the people here. Then I shared my plans for the mission with her. She was so enthusiastic that I brought her to see the vacant school building. She encouraged me, and even helped me put together a few corporate sponsors. Then she got sick, and I had to put the project on hold. When she died six months later, she left most of her estate to me. I'm sure she expected me to use it on the mission. But my parents were against the idea from the first minute they heard about my plans—''

''Because they were concerned about you being down here?''

Angel shook her head. ''No. They love to misquote the scriptures. 'The poor will always be with us.' That leaves them free to donate very publicly to charity, but not consider dirtying their hands by actually coming into contact with the people who need help. Their charity is all about show—and tax deductions.''

Greg frowned. ''So they didn't support you at all?''

''Are you kidding?'' Greg was surprised by the bitterness in her tone. ''They nearly sabotaged me. Just after Gran's lawyer informed me that she'd left the bulk of her estate to me, I found out that the school building was still available. I had the money from the estate transferred to my savings account, and I made a down payment. My account was in my uncle's bank. With his help, my father emptied my account right before settlement. He never said a word. My parents just sat back and watched me plan.''

''You must have been devastated. Couldn't you force them to return it?''

''Father told me that he'd spent it already. He said he'd suffered financial reversals and had been counting on the money he'd assumed Gran would leave to my mother. If I'd made an issue of it, my uncle, my father, and possibly my mother, would have been arrested. I couldn't do it. But the worst part is that it was all a lie.''

Greg's frown deepened. That made no sense. ''Your father lied to protect your uncle?''

''Oh, no. Nothing so noble. It wasn't the first lie he'd told me. I'd lost count of the lies and half truths over the years. 'Of course you can come home from boarding school for the holidays.' Then the call would come. 'Oh, dear, you and your sister will be much happier at Gran's for Christmas. Daddy and I will be so busy entertaining his clients that we won't have any time for you.''

Her tone grew even more bitter as a cloud scudded across the moon. '''Of course we'll be at your play...your recital...your graduation.' 'Angelica, dear, we just can't drop everything to come all the way up there for only two hours.' I don't know why this time was the last straw. I had to scramble practically overnight, calling on the original corporate sponsors. I managed to get the mission going, but it was a near miss—and a lot more difficult than it had to be.''

She turned to him finally. ''Please understand. It isn't the money. If he'd asked—if he'd really needed it—I would certainly have given it to him to save my parents from bankruptcy. But it turns out that he couldn't tell me beforehand because there *were* no financial reversals. I found out that he'd spent the money on a yacht. It was just one more convenient lie.

''I don't want to miss them. I don't want to care. And even though I *do* still miss them and love them,

I just can't forgive them. I just can't let them back into my life.''

Greg gazed at her intently and squeezed her hand. As he reflected upon her words, his stomach turned to stone. She'd never forgive him all his lies, either. He didn't see a way to salvage this. He could probably count the time he had left with her in hours rather than in days. It seemed hopeless. *Please, Lord Jesus, find a way! Help me fix the mess I've made of this.*

Angelica stood and walked to the water's edge. She leaned her shoulder against an old gnarled oak. Its thinning branches let the moonlight through, when the clouds moved from in front of the full moon. It shone brightly in the black summer sky and reflected on the still river. She felt, rather than heard, Greg approach behind her. She turned, finally ready to face him, and, in fact, she needed to see his face.

Angelica gazed up into his moonlit face and she gasped, her eyes widening.

In the silvery light, a new, even more devastatingly handsome Greg stood before her. He'd pulled his golden hair back at his nape and shaved off his scraggly beard. She'd known that he was handsome under all that hair, and had imagined that the beard hid a lot, but she hadn't let her imagination stretch this far. His deep-set eyes and high cheekbones were in perfect symmetry with a slightly square jaw and determined chin. His lips, now minus the fringe overshadowing them, were full and sensual. It was a strong face that belonged in the pages of women's magazines the world over. One of the old masters might have used him as a model for Michael the Archangel as he banished the fallen angels from heaven.

So now she knew that the man she was already desperately in love with had an unforgettable face to match his strong, gentle disposition. His absence that day had been nearly unbearable, which left her feeling desolate and utterly selfish, because she'd known that he'd gone to visit his family in a time of personal turmoil. Her pride and her vow not to pressure him had kept her from telling him the full truth. She did miss her family, but it had been *his* absence that had sent her emotions spiraling down into utter gloom.

Angelica reached up and cupped his smooth cheek, trying desperately to think of something to say. But then he put his hand over hers and turned his lips into her palm. All rational thought fled when she saw the desperate look in his eyes. Her arms, of their own volition, curled around his neck.

His free hand slid to her waist, and he drew her closer. They stared at each other for a couple of charged moments before his head dipped, blotting out the moonlight. Then his lips met hers, sending her senses reeling.

"You're so beautiful," he whispered against her lips as he broke the kiss, his voice deep and husky on the summer breeze. Her breath caught at the expression shining in his eyes. If she had to put a name to it, she could only call it love. "If it was just surface beauty, I could walk away," he continued. "But it's not. It goes all the way to your heart and soul."

"Why do you want to walk away?" She put her hand on his heart, feeling its wild pounding. "Why do I feel as if you're running from me when you don't want to any more than I do?''

He moved his hands to her shoulders, holding her gently but firmly. "Because you're so important to me. I don't want to mess this up." He cupped her cheek the way she had his. "I can't be near you and not want more than this. I can't sleep, knowing you're upstairs. So close, yet so far. I won't dishonor you or the Lord by asking for more, but I couldn't offer you anything else right now." He swallowed with apparent difficulty. "Angel, there are so many things that are still…unresolved in my life. Things about me that I can't talk about. Not yet. And I'm afraid because when I do, you'll be the one running. I'm afraid because when that happens, it's going to rip my heart out."

"But I'd never—"

Greg put his index finger on her lips. "Sh! Don't make a promise when you don't know what you're promising. The reason I keep pulling back is that I don't want to hurt you." He replaced his finger with his lips. Arms banding her back, he held her tightly against the hard wall of his chest. His kiss spun them instantly into a vortex of longing such as Angelica had never known could exist. Breathless, he broke away and stuffed his hands into the front pockets of his jeans. "I think I'd better get you home. Being here like this isn't a good idea."

"Because of the Judges?" she asked, still completely bemused by the alien feelings and needs zinging through her.

"No." He laughed shortly, tucked her arm in his, and turned them away from the river. "Because you're walking, talking, breathing temptation, Angelica DeVoe. And I want you behind locked doors and chaperoned by fifteen men, twenty women and—what's the latest count?—thirteen kids under eighteen?''

She cast a wry, sidelong glance at him. "Funny, I feel oddly complimented to be such a test of willpower for you."

"You aren't helping," he growled.

Angelica felt a giggle bubble to the surface. "Sorry."

"You don't sound very sorry."

"If it's any consolation, I feel the same way about you," she quipped.

Angelica heard Greg's breath hiss between his teeth and felt guilty for teasing him—until she found herself in his arms, being kissed again with a tender but desperate edge that made her feel cherished and needed.

Minutes later, as they entered the darkened mission, Angelica wondered how she'd managed to walk home when her feet felt as if they'd never touched the ground.

Chapter Thirteen

⌒‿

Greg stood back as Angel unlocked her door. Even as he told himself that kissing her, and once again revealing even a portion of his feelings for her, would be wrong, she turned from the partially opened door. Her emerald eyes had an adorable glazed look. Seeing that—knowing that—destroyed his resolve, and he found himself reaching for her. One more simple kiss before he left her. One more stolen moment before he faced the rest of his life without her.

But there was nothing simple about it when she melted into his arms and curled hers around his neck, holding on to him for dear life—the same way he held on to her. He'd never been more tempted to throw aside the principles of a lifetime. Then Angel let go of his neck and move her arms between them, forcing him back to sanity. Turmoil and a hint of fear had replaced the disorientation he'd seen in her gaze before he'd kissed her again.

Fear? Of him? Nothing had ever hurt more. ''Are

you afraid of me?'' he asked, praying he'd been wrong, dreading the answer but needing to hear the truth anyway.

She shook her head. ''Don't be silly. I'm afraid of me because I never understood before.''

''Understood?''

''Adam and Jean Ann, and all the others. How they could be so foolish. How they could take such a chance, knowing it was wrong. You can't stay. I can't—''

Greg silenced her with his fingertips pressed to her soft lips. ''I'm not asking to,'' he told her, trailing his fingers across her cheek, memorizing the softness of her skin for later. Determinedly he put that lonely ''later'' from his mind. He wouldn't ruin a second of the time he had with her with more dark thoughts.

Angel blushed. ''Oh, I must sound—''

''Sh-sh,'' he cut in. ''I think you sound just right. It's just that I have no intention of asking. Principles aren't principles if you break them when it's convenient. I know it and you know it.''

''Then why are you in my apartment?''

Greg looked around, stunned. How did I get in here? he wondered.

He grinned, feeling decidedly sheepish as he admitted the truth. ''I have no idea how we got inside. Do you?''

She shook her head, grinning now, too. Then they both started laughing. ''I guess that's why it's called temptation,'' she said, recovering before he did.

Greg looked into her shining eyes and quickly took a giant step backward into the hall. ''With a capital *T*. I'd better get outta here. See you tomorrow, sweetheart. Hope your birthday turned out okay. Sleep well.'' He turned and hurried away, feeling conflicted. They were so good together. He'd left her smiling— a far cry from the way he'd found her. They were like two halves of a whole.

Which means, he thought, you'll be half a person by the end of the week when the lid blows off this powder keg you've been sitting on since you first saw her. *Please, Jesus. Do something!*

An incessant ringing dragged Angelica out of a deep hard-won sleep. She slapped the top of her alarm clock, but the ringing continued. She forced her gritty eyes open to focus on the clock that refused to be quiet.

Ten o'clock?

She never slept till ten. Blinking, sure the numbers would change, Angelica bolted upright when they stayed stubbornly fixed on the same time. Then her sleep-fogged mind realized that it was the phone ringing. She grappled for it. ''Hello.''

''Angelica, it's Tracy.''

''Tracy?''

A musical laugh floated from the phone. ''Your sister, Tracy. I know you must be surprised to hear from me. I wanted to wish you a happy birthday. I know I'm a day late, but I spent yesterday at July Jam.''

Angelica's heart picked up its beat. *Please let this mean she's accepted You, Lord Jesus.* ''All day?'' she asked cautiously.

''My life seems so pointless. I remembered how you changed your life, and I wanted to understand how. And now I think I do. It wasn't you who changed it at all, was it?''

"It was Jesus."

"Yeah, that's what I thought. I haven't decided what to do about the things Joe Conway said, but I'm going back tonight. I wanted you to know. I haven't said anything to Mother or Daddy yet. Not until I think about it some more. I don't want them influencing me. I was never as strong as you."

"If you need to talk, call me anytime. You know this was never about me and you. It was about our parents and the way they live. And I'll pray for you, Tracy."

"I knew you'd say that." Tracy laughed, sounding young and exuberant. "It's why I called. Thanks. Well, I have to run. I'll call you."

"Have a good time, Tracy. I love you."

"I love you too, big sister. 'Bye."

Angelica flopped back on the bed and grinned. Today was already looking up.

When the phone rang in her office just after lunch, Angelica plucked it out of the cradle with enthusiasm.

"Where is your sister?"

"Mother?"

"Don't 'Mother' me. And don't try to act innocent. I know you talked her into going to some evangelical tent meeting somewhere. One of her friends called and told me where she and a couple of others had gone. I demand you tell me where this July Jam thing is being held!"

Angelica took a deep breath. "Tracy called me earlier to tell me her plans, but going to the event was her idea entirely. It's being held at Veterans Stadium in Philadelphia. Why? Are you planning to go down there and drag her home?''

''Actually, we had thought about doing just that. I'm not losing another daughter to some Jesus cult.''

''I don't belong to a cult. Jesus is a person, not a cult. Please, don't go after her. She needs to hear the truth and make up her own mind.''

''Your truth, you mean. Truth. Truth. Truth. You're like a broken record and no one can talk to you. No one.''

Angelica pulled the phone away from her ear in time to avoid the explosive sound of her mother hanging up on her. Again. She shook off the melancholy feeling that started to descend on her. She would not let her mother steal her joy. Her little sister was at a crusade—the same crusade where she herself had been saved several years earlier. She closed her eyes and prayed that Tracy would make the right decision. Then she went in search of Greg. She wanted to share her news with him, and he'd been flitting around all day, too busy to stop and talk for even a minute. The man had more energy than a nuclear power plant.

Angelica stopped setting up chairs to listen to the band practice. She never tired of hearing Greg's voice raised in song. Looking at him, the peace of the Lord shining from him, it was hard to believe that this was the same edgy, anxious man who'd prowled the mission and the neighborhood for the last few days.

And she'd thought that he was never still *before* the night he'd found her in the park! In the last four days she'd gotten a firsthand lesson in perpetual motion. He scrubbed, patched, painted with a nearly frantic drive that made her uneasy. If he kept up this determined pace, within days there wouldn't be anything but emergencies left to deal with. He was working himself out of a job.

And then a disturbing idea occurred to her: Maybe that's what he's trying to do. Maybe he's planning to leave.

Angelica pushed the unbidden thought away as she sank into a chair and closed her eyes. He couldn't kiss her the way he had and not love her. But did that mean that he wouldn't leave? Or that he felt he had to? After all, he did say that he had nothing to offer her yet.

Yet.

Did that mean that at some time in the future he *would* have something to offer? But only if he felt he could, she reminded herself. Did he need to leave in order to deal with the part of his past that he thought she wouldn't be able to accept? That would certainly hurt and be difficult for her. But as long as she knew that it was what he needed and that he'd be back, she could accept his decision. She loved him enough to let him go. What worried her was that he might feel he had to leave because of the two of them and what they felt for each other, even though he needed to be at a place like the mission in order to be whole again.

They hadn't talked about the desire that flared between them when they were alone. But then, with Greg running around like Super Handyman, when had they been alone with each other long enough that they *could* talk about it?

They still shared meals, but there were always other mission residents within hearing range. Those weren't the times to discuss something as private as the kisses they'd shared on her birthday. Instead, they talked about their days: Greg's filled with plaster, paint, glue and tar paper; hers, with counseling, fund-raising, and helping residents find jobs.

Greg and the band moved into an upbeat song. "Our God Is an Awesome God" was a particular favorite of hers. Angelica opened her eyes and grinned, when Greg started clowning around with the band, quickening the beat of the contemporary Christian hit. Though the band had performed it before, no one had been able to sing the refrain at as fast a beat as did the original artist. The band caught up quickly, and all the residents who'd been helping to put up chairs in the gym stopped and joined in on the chorus, applauding enthusiastically when the set ended.

When practice was over, Greg set the guitar he'd been playing off to the side of the stage, and approached her. "You should feel very guilty, you know," she told him.

His eyes widened. "Guilty?"

"Remember the Sermon on the Mount? I'd say you've been hiding your light under a bushel for years."

"That's not how it started out. But plans change." Greg shrugged, but the gesture wasn't as careless as she was sure he'd meant it to look.

"They changed when your brother died." It wasn't a question. In light of the conversation he'd had with Brian in the ER, it was the only thing that made sense. The loss of his brother had put Greg on a new path— the wrong path, from what she could see.

"He was my best friend. And yet I didn't know. Didn't see."

"That he was sick? Greg, how could you have known there was something wrong?"

"Because his sickness was the same sickness that's destroying North Riverside. My brother died of a drug overdose. I shared a room with him, and I never saw it."

Angelica took a quick shocked breath. A brother lost to drugs. She could only imagine the pain he'd felt. "And that changed your plans? How? What did you see for your life before?"

Greg shrugged. "I'd thought about being a pastor, but when I couldn't even help my own brother, I knew I'd been wrong."

"Maybe you weren't. Maybe what happened with your brother had nothing to do with God's plan for you."

Greg stiffened and put his hand over his shirt pocket. He looked suddenly distracted. "Maybe. I'll think about it. But right now I have to go."

Angelica frowned. "Go?"

He'd already begun to move toward the exit. "I left a mess to clean up in the basement. Paint rollers and brushes to wash." He waved. "See you at dinner."

Greg hotfooted it out of the gym and headed for the basement, his cell phone vibrating in his pocket. "Yeah," he said after hitting the Answer button on his way down the basement steps.

"It's Jim. We've got all the warrants. It's a go for

the morning, but Torres wants to meet with you beforehand. He wants your input."

"Not now. I need to be here at seven-thirty. Angelica's counting on me to lead worship. Tonight's guest pastor always draws a big crowd from his own church. I have to be here. Two-thirds of the people who come will be strangers. It's too dangerous for her. Anyone could get close to her."

"No problem. I've got a lot of coordination to handle in the next several hours before we're ready for you. I'll pick you up outside the mission around four in the morning. The operation should be all but over by the time I drop you back there, so it ought to be safe. We'll be in place and ready to go by dawn."

Greg let out a deep sigh. "That sounds like an answer to a prayer—and a court sentence at the same time. I dread facing Angel with the truth, but if I have to wait much longer, I'll unravel at the seams."

"Tomorrow you can start putting it all back together, buddy. See you later."

Angelica came out of her bathroom, the thirst that had awakened her quenched. She lifted her heavy hair off her neck and back, where it clung to her sweaty skin. The muggy July heat was unbearable in her apartment even though it was the middle of the night.

For privacy's sake, she'd chosen to tuck her rooms in the front corner of the third floor but all the heat in the building rose, turning her little haven into an oven for three months of the year. Though she felt better after tying her hair up and changing her nightgown, there was no air stirring through the windows and thus little chance of her getting back to sleep. It looked as if her noisy, old air conditioner was the lesser of two evils tonight. The rattle had to be better than the sensation of melting in her bed.

As Angelica reach up to close the front window, she saw movement near the front steps. It was Greg, his golden hair glinting in the moonlight. She was about to call out to him when a car—the same car that had dropped him off the morning after Adam was shot—pulled up in front of the mission. Greg stood without hesitation, loped over and got in. Angelica shrugged, wondering if it was Brian. She hoped there was nothing wrong in their family.

Just after the car bearing Greg rounded the corner, another car that sat in the shadow of a huge sycamore sparked to life and followed. Angelica frowned. There was an awful lot of activity on the street at four in the morning—even for North Riverside.

"Call me when you've got everyone in custody. And do me a favor—let Hudson and DeVega know who I am. It has to make them feel a little better about all this to know that one less criminal walked. I'm in the same boat as they are right now. I mean, if you can't trust your own, who can you trust? And what's all this about, anyway, if the system can get this corrupted?"

"Try to see the big picture, Greg," Jim urged. "This is only one district of the city. There are a lot of Hudsons and DeVegas on the streets, and there are several Greg Petersons, too. Don't let a few rotten apples sour you on the whole department.

"Why don't you go straighten things out with Angelica? Try to remember all the good this operation is going to do for the people of this area. We've got enough on the Judges to convict nearly all of them. I'm heading over to the Precinct house now to help with the IAD arrests. In ten minutes this neighborhood will be cleaner than it's been in years. You did that, Greg. And it was you last night who finally linked that informant—the one who named Angelica as a trafficker at the outset of this—to Judge Whiting. I'll stop by in a couple of hours to see how it all goes.''

Greg nodded and stepped out of the car. Looking back at Jim as he sped away to the coming confrontation at the Third Precinct house, he knew his friend was right. He just couldn't quite get his heart around the concept. He still felt as if the last six years of his life had been wasted. It was difficult to face the fact that after thinking all along that he knew exactly what he was doing with his life, he'd suddenly come to a place where he felt adrift on a sea of doubt and disillusionment.

He looked up the mission steps, dreading the coming encounter with Angel. He was tempted to just pack and leave. But it would be cowardly, and in the long run would hurt no less than not knowing whether she would have forgiven him his lies.

It was just past dawn, so the main room was deserted except for Angel, who sat behind the desk. She appeared troubled when she looked up at him. He approached the desk, knowing what a man on the way to his own execution must feel like.

''Is everything all right?'' she asked. ''I saw you leave around four. Was that your brother who picked you up?''

"No, he's a friend. My best friend. His name's Jim Lovell."

"I didn't know you had a friend." She blushed and smiled sheepishly. "Oh, my. I guess that sounds insulting. Pay me no mind. I'm a little rattled. Remember that thing I found that you thought was a button? Look." She handed him another of the bugs he'd planted. "Emanuel found this one in the kitchen a few minutes ago. He thinks it's a bug. You know, a high-tech listening device. Maybe Antonio wasn't passing information, or maybe he planted them."

Greg closed his eyes, then shook his head. "Angel, we need to talk. There are some things I have to tell you. The things about me that I wasn't free to tell you before…" He hesitated and took a deep fortifying breath. "I'm hoping you can forgive me now that I'm allowed to tell you."

Angelica frowned, looking up at him with confusion and something that might have been fear written on her precious features. "Allowed? I thought you weren't *able* to talk about what was bothering you. As in…it was too painful. And what has this to do with the Judges bugging the mission."

Greg shook his head. "One thing at a time. First, I was under orders not to tell anyone—especially you—who I am."

She stiffened and stood. "Who you are?" she echoed, her face frozen with dread.

"My name isn't Peters. It's Peterson."

Her eyes narrowed and went cold. "Under orders? From whom, and why especially me?"

"There's no easy way to say this. I'm Detective Greg Peterson. Narcotics Division. Riverside P.D."

"And why especially me?" Her voice was now as glacial as her eyes.

Greg looked down at his feet, willing them to turn away. To leave. To run. It was going to be as bad as he'd feared all along. But she deserved to know, because, though she was angry, she was hurt as well. And he'd hurt her. So he looked back up at the punishment her angry eyes doled out. "Because when I came here, you were the chief suspect. It was my job to get evidence that you were trafficking. The bugs were mine."

"Get out."

"Angel."

"Don't call me that! Just pack and get out."

The cell phone in his pocket vibrated. Not now! No, he wouldn't answer it. This was his life here. "Please, let me explain."

"Explain that you haven't once told me the truth from the first minute I laid eyes on you? That you spied on me? That your clothes, your life, your faith have all been lies?"

"No. I told you the truth about everything I could. Especially about my faith and my feelings for you. I knew right away that you were innocent, and I proved it. You're in the clear and—"

"Well, thank you, Detective Peterson. Now you can go back to your life, and I'll go back to mine. I'd like you gone. Preferably five minutes ago!"

Greg put his hand out in supplication. "Would you please listen?"

Angel came out from behind the counter and stalked down the hall toward his room. Greg followed close on her heels. He had to make her listen.

"There were reasons. This turned out to be bigger than you can imagine. I had to stay to keep you safe, and lying about who I am was the only way. You have to listen! You can't do this to us!"

"There is no *us*, Detective," she snapped, not slowing a bit.

Desperate, watching the only part of his life that he was sure about disintegrate before his eyes, Greg grabbed her and spun her into his arms. "Then what's this?" he asked, and pressed his lips onto hers. She melted for a split second, then shoved him hard. Greg let go.

"Unimportant is what that is. I've spent my life caring about liars. I don't intend to continue on a path of destruction, or to listen to any more lies from you. If you won't pack your things, then I will." She turned away and pushed open the door to his room.

It was one of those instants when action decelerates into slow motion. When seconds seem to last minutes. When your brain goes into overdrive, processing data and sending signals so quickly that time loses definition. Angel shoved on the door and rushed forward. In his peripheral vision, Greg caught a shadow inside the room, and the hair at the back of his neck prickled. She looked back at him, and the shadow moved toward her. He dove into the room after her, just as Officer John Worth leveled his gun.

Panic was a living thing in Worth's eyes. And there's nothing more dangerous than a gun in the hands of someone in a panic. Greg didn't think about it for even a split second. He launched himself in front of Angel, putting his own body between her and Worth.

Then two gunshots echoed in the room.

Chapter Fourteen

It all happened so fast.

Greg suddenly yelled, "No!" as he hurtled into the room and leapt in front of her. Was that desperation in his voice? Before the question had fully formed in Angelica's mind, two explosions echoed in the room. Greg jerked backward and, as he did, pivoted to face her. Her brain had scarcely processed the look of alarm on his face, when he pushed her to the floor. She landed on her back with Greg over her, his weight forcing the air out of her lungs.

There was no time to even try to recover her breath. A voice shouted, "IAD. Don't move a muscle." Move? she thought. I can't even breathe! But when several sets of feet thundered past them, she realized that she and Greg weren't who the men were focused on. From under Greg's shoulder, Angelica saw a tall blond man quickly handcuff a uniformed policeman who'd apparently been in Greg's room. At the same time, another man started reading the officer his rights, while a third, using a cell phone, reported that the officer was in custody. IAD, she thought fuzzily. Internal Affairs. So they were policemen arresting another officer?

Angelica tried to get up, but Greg still had her pinned to the floor, shielding her upper body with his own. She could hardly breathe. "I think…it's safe now," she gasped, but he showed no sign of moving. The blond cop glanced toward them then, and his eyes widened. He grabbed the cell phone from the man using it and shouted, "Officer down!"

Angelica frowned. What officer was down? Then the blonde and another uniformed cop were hovering over her and Greg. And her heart stuttered in understanding before her mind could fully grasp the horrible truth. The cop in uniform gripped Greg by the shoulder and rolled him carefully off her. Greg's breathing was labored and his head lolled to one side. Scrambling to her knees, she supported Greg's neck, then looked up into the face of the big blond cop, expecting reassurance. She found none. He looked as stricken as she felt. They both helped the officer in uniform gently roll Greg completely to his back.

Angelica looked on mutely as both men worked at the buttons of his shirt. She noticed for the first time that blood had already pooled on the floor—Greg's blood.

How could everything change that quickly? she thought hazily. Had even a minute gone by since she'd flung open the door?

Tears filled her eyes. How could she ever live with the knowledge that while she'd shouted that she wanted him out of her life, Greg had thrown himself between her and a gunman, taking a bullet meant for her? This was all her fault.

The big blond cop looked up at the one with the cell phone. "It's bad. Tell dispatch he took two hits. One on his chest. The other's lower in the abdomen and bleeding badly. Tell them to get that ambulance over here fast." He looked back at Greg. "Greg, it's Jim. Can you hear me? Come on, buddy. Open your eyes and look at me."

"Greg," Angelica called, finally finding her voice. He moved his head toward her a bit, and his eyelids flickered but didn't open.

"He heard you. Talk to him," Jim ordered abruptly.

She stroked Greg's hair. "You're going to be fine. Can you hear me?"

Greg's eyes flickered, as Emanuel tore into the room with clean towels. The uniformed cop moved aside, and the cook dropped to his knees, praying furiously under his breath. Then he switched to dire threats, should Greg even consider dying. As Emanuel pressed down hard on the wounds, Greg's eyes flew open and he drew a pain-filled breath through gritted teeth. Then his gaze rose to meet hers. "Hated lying to you. Have to believe me."

"I do." She wiped her eyes, trying to dry her tears so she could see him clearly. "It's okay. I overreacted. Don't worry about it."

He grimaced. "Guilty...so guilty. Lied to you...for weeks and weeks. Didn't mean to...hurt you."

"I was *wrong*. You did what you had to do. I know that now. I probably knew it then." *Then*, she thought. *Then* was hardly five full minutes ago.

Greg grinned weakly. "Saved my angel, though."

"Yeah, buddy. You sure did," Jim said.

But Greg only had eyes for her. "Couldn't save Jessie. Tommy, either." Tears filled his beautiful, pain-glazed, blue eyes. "Always failed before. Couldn't let him hurt you. So sorry *I* did." He lifted his hand shakily to caress her cheek, then his eyes rolled back in his head and his hand dropped heavily into her lap.

Angelica grabbed his hand with both of hers and brought it to her lips. "You didn't mean to hurt me. I know you didn't."

"Stay with us, buddy," Jim commanded.

"Jim," Greg whispered. He opened his eyes again, narrowing them as if it took a determined effort to focus.

Jim grasped Greg's other hand. "I'm here. Take it easy. We had an ambulance and paramedics standing by. They'll be here any second. You're going to be fine."

"Not too sure…this time. If not, take…care…my angel." He closed his eyes and his breath rattled oddly.

"Greg!" Angelica cried.

"Don't give up!" Jim commanded, as Emanual ordered, "Don't you dare leave us!"

But Greg was beyond responding.

The paramedics, their equipment clattering, rushed into the small, stuffy room not a second later, and ordered everyone out. Angelica shook her head. She wasn't leaving Greg. She couldn't. Instead, she laid his hand on the floor and scrambled to a position above his head, where she wouldn't be in the way.

Where she could be near him. She closed her eyes and prayed furiously for his life.

Afterward she would understand why they'd tried to get her to leave. Greg had not just fallen into unconsciousness.

His heart had stopped.

She heard the two paramedics shouting directions to each other about starting CPR. Finally, she heard the miraculous words, "We've got a heartbeat. Let's move to transport before he goes south again. The trauma team and an OR are standing by at Saint Al's."

Two ambulance attendants wheeled a gurney into the room, and as they moved Greg from the floor onto the gurney, Jim Lovell stood by her side, his grim, accusing countenance anything but comforting.

"He's ready," one of the ambulance attendants called out.

"Then let's roll," the other paramedic responded.

"We'll follow them in my car," Jim said, and grabbed her arm. Angelica would be eternally grateful to him, because she might have simply stood there in a stupor, watching them wheel the man she loved off to an uncertain and possibly very short future. She couldn't seem to digest it all, but she knew reality would set in soon. She also knew that no matter what the outcome, the last quarter of an hour would visit her in her nightmares for years to come.

All it had taken was a second to tear her life apart.

The ride to the hospital was accomplished with Jim Lovell sparing her nothing but a hard stare before he reached for the ignition and drove through the neighborhood, practically glued to the bumper of the ambulance.

Angelica did the only thing for Greg that she knew how to do. She prayed. Prayers of desperation. Prayers of petition. Prayers of supplication. Prayers for wisdom for the people trying to save him.

The jostling of the car as Lovell pulled to a stop behind the ambulance in the ER driveway brought Angelica back to the temporal world. And as she jumped out to see if Greg had survived the ride, she prayed the hardest prayer she'd ever prayed. ''Thy will be done, Lord Jesus,'' she said aloud, as the ambulance doors sprung open.

Lovell shot her another hard glare, as the attendants told them that Greg was hanging on—but just barely. This is all your fault, his look said, Don't you dare tell God that He can have him.

Angelica turned away from Lovell to follow behind the gurney and the paramedics who shouted information about Greg to the trauma team. A doctor directed the actions of his team as he listened to the paramedic's report. She stood just inside the ER, dazed by all the activity, as Greg was transferred to an ER bed and he then disappeared behind a wall of bodies.

A hand on her shoulder yanked her attention away from the chaotic scene. Angelica turned her head. ''Brian,'' she choked, and bit her lip, fighting tears. She stared up into a face painfully like Greg's, then went into his waiting arms.

''I know this looks bad, but he's a fighter,'' Brian told her.

''I know. He's a fighter, but he had trouble

breathing right away and his heart stopped at the mission."

"His lungs were collapsing. They'll insert a chest tube and reinflate his lungs. That'll give him relief right away. We've got an operating room standing ready, and he'll be wheeled in any minute now. This is a terrific team. He's in good hands."

"Shouldn't you be in there helping?"

Brian shook his head. "I'm too close to this, but I'll go back in case they need an extra pair of hands." He steered her toward an old-fashioned-looking room dominated by forest-green marble on the floors and halfway up the walls. The rough plaster above the marble was painted institutional green. "You come on into the waiting room and try to relax. I'll bring out progress reports. In the meantime—" he hugged her again "—pray harder than you ever have."

She did just that until she heard Lovell using the pay phone just inside the waiting room. He told whoever he'd called that Greg was lucky there had been an ambulance standing by. What did he mean—standing by? He'd said the same thing to Greg. And now that she thought about that, she began to question all of what had happened at the mission. How had they known Worth was at the mission in Greg's room?

"How did you know to come to the mission?" she asked, when Lovell hung up the phone and turned in to the room. "You and the others seemed to appear out of the blue."

"Because Greg's been so worked up about your safety, we decided to have our men monitor the bugs at the mission until the operation was a wrap and the Judges had all been scooped up. We knew Greg had left that bug—the one you found in the conference room—in his room. They heard someone in his room, but at first they thought it was Greg. Then Worth's handheld radio squawked, and they knew it had to be one of our suspects from the Third. They alerted my team, and we got there as fast as we could. Unfortunately, too late for Greg.''

There was an edge to his voice, and she understood his cold attitude. He blamed her as much as she did herself. ''You heard our argument.''

''Not all of it. When the team called to tell me about the suspect in Greg's room, I heard your voice in the background telling Greg to pack and get out. I called him to tell him you were about to send him into an ambush, but he ignored his cell phone. He was too busy trying to get you to listen to reason.''

Stricken by the ruthlessness of his assessment, Angelica closed her eyes, accepting his harsh judgment. ''You're right, I did send him into that room. In fact, what you don't know is that I opened the door, and at least the first bullet that hit Greg was meant for me. So you see, there's no way you can make me feel worse about this than I do already.''

Brian came in and shot Lovell a quelling glare. ''Greg cares about Angelica. We have no right to judge what happened between them.'' He turned to Angelica. ''Greg regained consciousness for a few seconds. He called your name, and I let him know you were here. They've taken him up to OR. Come on,'' he said, then took her arm. ''You can wait for news upstairs in the OR lounge. I'll come out and report every once in a while. My parents are on their way in with Greg's boss. They'll come up to the waiting room when they arrive.''

Once Angelica and Brian reached the room, a volunteer gave her change for the pay phone so she could call the mission. Emanuel and the rest of the residents had gathered in the gym to pray. She promised to let them know when Greg was out of surgery. Then she sank into a corner chair, trying to ignore Jim Lovell and his resentment. Greg didn't need Jim's anger— or her guilt. Guilt had apparently ruled Greg's life for years, and, from what she could see, it had done him no good at all. What Greg needed was prayer.

But a few minutes later, her thoughts strayed. She turned her gaze on Lovell. Though he and Greg were very different, there were striking similarities. She saw in him the same kind of discontent that ate at Greg. But even though it was plain to see that there were still things that disturbed him, Greg had found some measure of peace during his weeks at the mission. He really *had* needed her help, then. He hadn't been pretending about that, at least.

A commotion at the OR advocate's desk drew her attention. "How's my officer?" asked a man with salt-and-pepper hair. He wore a blue suit that didn't quite meet across his stomach. She assumed that he was Greg's boss, because he'd arrived with an older couple who couldn't be anyone but Greg's parents.

Though easily twice Greg's age and more white-haired than blond, the man with his arm around a small woman had clearly handed down almost every one of his genes to his sons. The woman seemed fragile, but when Angelica looked at her closely, she saw Greg's laser-blue eyes staring back at her. If the expression on her face was any indication, Greg's mother was a fountain of strength.

Lovell bounded to his feet and went to join them, but Angelica didn't move. She felt that she had no right. They were here, looking sick with worry all because she'd distracted their son from his job.

It should have been Angelica lying in that operating room fighting for her life—not Greg. Greg might not need her guilt, but she felt it all the same. She shook her head, realizing that she'd stopped praying and had begun to wallow again.

Before Angelica could turn her thoughts back to prayer, Greg's mother sat down in the chair next to her. "I'm Thomasina Peterson. You must be Greg's Angel. You look exactly the way he described you. Are you all right, dear?"

Angelica shook her head, tears blurring her vision. "It's all my fault...I'm so sorry."

Greg's mother frowned and patted Angelica's hand. "I very much doubt that this was your fault—"

"You don't understand. We had a terrible argument when he told me who he really was. All I could see were his lies—"

"After you were hurt," said Thomasina, "he called me and told me that he was worried about keeping secrets."

"—During the argument, I rushed into his room, and then he was there, pushing me to the floor. A gun went off and— It was my fault. He was trying to protect me."

"And thank the Lord he did. Greg wouldn't have wanted it any other way. But as for whose fault this is, I would say that other than the man with the gun, it's the judge's fault.''

Angelica frowned. ''The judge? Don't you mean the Judges?—the gang that's been threatening me?''

''No dear. Apparently a judge and several of the local Precinct officers were involved with that gang. Captain Harris says it was the judge's gang, and that the Precinct captain was apparently being blackmailed into silence by the judge.''

Angelica glanced up at Greg's boss as he approached them. ''Which judge?'' she asked.

''Harold Whiting,'' Harris growled in reply. From the expression on his face, she could tell that he was very angry. Her gaze flicked to Lovell, who sat nearby, and she wondered if Captain Harris's anger was directed at her or at Judge Whiting.

Unable to sit still with so many emotions and thoughts bombarding her, she stood and walked to the windows overlooking a courtyard. A veil suddenly lifted from more than just the last months. So much of the last two years made sense. It was no small wonder that the neighborhood had gone from bad to worse. No small wonder that significant arrests hadn't been made, and that the few that had been made went nowhere in court. And the governor's task force that Whiting supposedly petitioned had probably never heard about the problems in North Riverside.

And more recent events took on a new perspective. Greg's disgust with officers Worth and Gates for instance. They'd botched Sam Jackson's arrest on purpose. Seeing two trained officers make such blatant errors must have made Greg extremely suspicious, as well as angry. And then there was his unsettling depression the morning after Judge Whiting had released him. It hadn't been Greg's night in jail, but his abrupt release, that had upset him. The judge must have thought Greg was guilty; he'd been protecting what he must have assumed was a customer. She'd thought at the time that Greg had looked as if an integral part of his inner being had been wounded. Now she knew it had been. She hurt for him, having worked for so many years to try to make a difference—only to uncover such deeply entrenched corruption.

Angelica turned at the sound of Captain Harris's voice. "I'm sorry we ordered Greg not to tell you who he was. If we'd listened to his assessment of your character when he first discounted you as a suspect, he would have been free to tell you almost from the beginning."

"Greg had a few days when he could have told you," Lovell added, "but you were recuperating, and he worried about upsetting you." He was looking toward them, resentment still rife in his tone.

Harris shot Lovell a perplexed look, then spoke again. "The Sunday after you were hurt, we put you back on the suspect list when you gave Greg a marked fifty-dollar bill. Greg didn't know how you came by the money, but he always believed you were innocent."

"I came by it when Judge Whiting put it in the collection," Angelica said, anger warring with guilt. Guilt with fear. Fear with pain.

Harris's eyebrows dipped in the center of his forehead, forming a deep *V*. "Would you mind telling me why you sound so sure that it was Whiting's money you gave to Greg? We've only been speculating on that. We can't prove it.''

Anger filled her when Angelica remembered that night. ''Because, Captain, I saw Judge Whiting put it in the basket. He made a great production of it, in fact. And believe me, there was no one else in that room who could have afforded to put fifty dollars in the collection. And since my cook and I count the collection together, I can tell you it was the only fifty-dollar bill we received.''

''Now don't anybody jump down my throat. I'm only playing devil's advocate here. How can you be sure it wasn't Detective Peterson himself who put it in there? It's a question any defense attorney will ask.''

''Because, Captain, at no time was Greg near the basket that was passed. His arms just aren't that long. He led worship and presented the message that night from the stage in full view of everyone who attended.''

''Would you testify to all of that?''

''Considering what that man has done, you couldn't stop me. To think of what that hypocrite has done to our community these past two years. It makes me so mad!''

''We all feel that way, Ms. DeVoe,'' the captain said. ''But you'll have a chance for revenge when they all have their day in court.''

''I don't want revenge. And I don't want to think about them and their day in court, Captain. I just want someone to come out here and tell me Greg's going to be all right.''

Greg's father walked forward and sat on Angelica's

other side. "I'm Greg's father. I'm sorry we have to meet this way, but I am glad to meet the woman who got Greg thinking about where he was going."

"It's good to meet you, too, Mr. Peterson."

"Call me Bud. Mr. Peterson was my father."

Angelica remembered almost those exact words falling from Greg's lips, not long after he showed up at the mission. She needed to talk about that Greg—not the Greg whose job it had been to risk his life to expose corruption and end the sale of drugs.

"Greg told me about your cabin," she told his father, and felt a wistful smile tip her lips upward. "Those fishing weekends meant a lot to him. Even when he was hiding his identity, he talked about his family. You're all an important part of his life."

Misty-eyed, Bud Peterson nodded. "Suppose we all pray for our boy now. There's plenty of time to think about all that's happened after he's on the mend."

Chapter Fifteen

"Mom. Dad," Brian said as he entered the waiting room two hours later. He knelt on one knee to hug his mother. Sober-faced, he slid into a chair in their midst, never letting go of Thomasina Peterson's hand. But he was clearly assessing his father. "How you doin', Dad?"

"Don't be wasting your time on me. I'll be fine as long as Greg is. But the waiting is tough."

Brian raked his hand through his hair in a very Greg-like gesture, and Angelica swore that she felt a pain in the region of her heart. "Well, there's no easy way to start this. He's very critical. The bullets don't look as if they permanently damaged any vital organs, but he lost a great deal of blood."

"Then why are you so grim? Please be honest," Greg's mother said.

Brian sighed. "It's the amount of blood he lost that has me the most concerned. There's a limit to how much we can replace without serious side effects. It's different in everyone, but Greg's straddling the line this time.''

"How much longer till we know?'' Lovell demanded. At first, Angelica thought it was impatience that put an edge to his tone, but there was too much coiled tension in his stormy gray eyes.

"He'll still be in there for a while. Most surgeries like this last a long time.''

"Well, then, would you stop sounding like a doctor and give us a guess at his chances,'' said Lovell.

Brian nodded, unruffled. "I can't make promises. You know that. Usually we give the family the most pessimistic view we can to prepare them for the worst but—'' he took a deep breath "—barring anything unforeseen, and considering how hard he's holding on, I think he'll make it through surgery okay. But it's all in the Lord's hands, Jim.''

"Don't. I don't want to hear that.''

"Jim, maybe you need to take a walk,'' Greg's father said, his voice calm, understanding. "You need to get away from here for a while, son. I know this feels like a nightmare replaying itself. I'll call you on your cell phone if there's anything at all to tell you.''

"No.'' Lovell paused, clearly trying to control his emotions. "I can do this. Maybe—maybe I'll just go move my car out of the ER lot. I'll be back. Greg…''

Greg's father looked tired and pale, but he was a tower of strength for them all. "Greg would understand if you needed to leave for a while,'' Mr. Peterson told Lovell.

Lovell stood and rammed his hands in his front pockets of his beige chinos, his broad shoulders hunched forward. "Yeah. Yeah, I guess he would. It's different, but the same." He shook his head and swallowed hard. "It isn't even that different though, is it? Greg's fighting for his life, and Jessie's still dead." Lovell turned and walked out, his gazed fixed on the marble tile at his feet.

"Hard to say who's in for a rougher time in the next couple of days—him or Greg," Brian said and took a deep breath. "Why don't you all go check out what the ptomaine palace downstairs is serving? It's getting near lunchtime, in case you haven't noticed, and I doubt any of you has eaten today. Bad as the cafeteria food is, it'll go quickly once the staff starts piling in for the lunch shifts. And you'll need to keep your strength up."

"And you, son?" Thomasina Peterson asked.

"Oh, I think I'll go look over Jerry North's shoulder for a while. Keep an eye on that big brother of mine." He sighed. "But first I'd better bite the bullet and call Joy. As big a pain as she is, for some unknown reason, Jim can talk to her."

"That's a good idea. He could use his sister right now."

"Poor Jim. Imagine having Joy as your only refuge." Brian shook his head and walked out.

Thomasina smiled faintly, as Brian walked out. "Brian and Joy have fought since she was in diapers," she explained to Angelica, then sighed. "At least some things never change."

Bud Peterson tensed his jaw as he looked around the room. "This room hasn't changed a bit, either. Jim's right. Sitting here like this in this room feels all too familiar."

Greg's mother nodded. "This must be so hard for poor Jim, after losing Jessie last time."

Angelica frowned. "*Jim* lost Jessie?" she asked.

"She and Jim were about to set a wedding date, dear. Who did you—? Greg? You thought Greg was in love with Jessie?"

Angelica nodded. "He never *said* he was more to her than a friend. But her death weighs so heavily on him, and he spoke of her with such love in his eyes that I thought they'd been more to each other than friends."

"Greg loved her very much, but like a sister. He was her partner, and he felt her loss deeply."

"Knowing that they were partners explains so much. Like why he might blame himself for her death."

"He blames himself for our Tom's death, as well," his mother said. "I hope Greg learns soon that police work isn't his calling, no matter how good he is at it."

Angelica smiled, but knew it was a wistful one. "I saw the same thing. If it helps, I think toward the end he'd begun to see it too. I know what he did share with me was *who* he really was—and what he wanted. I told Greg he would make a wonderful pastor. He has such inspiring insights into the Word. He said that it had been what he thought he wanted before his brother died. It could be again, if he could only let go of the guilt that sent him into police work in the first place."

"Mom. Dad. Go eat!" Brian called into the room as he passed by again.

"Would you like to come with us?" Bud asked.

Angelica shook her head. "No. As appetizing as Brian made the cafeteria sound, I couldn't eat a thing. I think I'll try the chapel for a while."

"That's a wonderful idea," Thomasina said. "We'll bring you up a little something, just in case you get hungry later. Maybe you'll be able to nibble."

Angelica walked toward the chapel, leaving Greg's parents at the elevators. The chapel was much the same as the rest of the hospital: old-fashioned and traditional in the best sense of the words. Marble. Substantial wooden pews. It had an atmosphere she needed right then. Solid as a rock. The Rock.

Angelica sat and closed her eyes, her thoughts winging upward. *Please, let him live. Please. I don't see how he could forgive me for the way I acted, but at least I'd know he's out there somewhere. Please.* Her prayer came down to that one word. *Please.* She could think of no other, so she said it over and over.

Only that one all-encompassing word flooded her thoughts. *Please.* It seemed to ask for all that was good. All that was merciful. All that was necessary for earthly happiness for her and so many others who loved Greg.

Please.

Angelica stood outside ICU, watching Greg through a glass wall. He lay still. So still. He'd yet to wake from the surgery that had saved his life. She would never forget the way Brian Peterson's voice had cracked when he'd rushed into the waiting room. "He made it! He's on his way to recovery. You can see him for a couple of minutes in about an hour.''

But that had been hours ago....

Angelica stepped into the ICU room, her stomach muscles knotted. The sounds within were both foreign and frightening, because the necessity of each pointed to Greg's precarious hold on life. A respirator pumped and hissed, clicking and clattering as it did the work of Greg's strained and damaged lungs. Monitors beeped and chattered, charting his progress in languages that were foreign to her ears.

Determinedly, she put one foot in front of the other. She longed to see his beloved face, but she was afraid, too—afraid she'd see death when she looked at him. The memory of those moments at the mission when he'd stopped breathing, when his heart had given up its valiant struggle, were ones she could never put aside for long.

But when she did look at him, she saw only the man she loved more than life itself. His bright eyes were closed now. His long, thick lashes were lying against cheekbones that were a bit more prominent than they'd been. His lips that so often were turned up in a wide smile were cracked and dry. His golden mane lay spread out on the white pillow. He was still and pale, but he didn't look beaten or defeated. Angelica could feel his strong, vital spirit fill the room.

''Greg,'' she said, taking his limp hand in hers. ''I know you can hear me. We need you to keep fighting. To keep running the race, no matter how impossible getting better may seem right now. Remember Psalm 46.'' Angelica opened the Bible his father had lent her, and read the Psalm aloud:

"'God is our refuge and strength, an ever-present help in trouble. Therefore we will not fear, though the earth give way and the mountains fall into the heart of the sea, though its waters roar and foam and the mountains quake with their surging.

"'There is a river whose streams make glad the city of God, the holy place where the Most High dwells. God is within her, she will not fall; God will help her at break of day. Nations are in uproar, kingdoms fall; He lifts his voice, the earth melts.

"'The Lord Almighty is with us; the God of Jacob is our fortress.'"

"Miss DeVoe, it's time," a nurse said from the doorway.

Angelica nodded. "Hold on to that, Greg," she said, giving his strong hand a gentle squeeze. "No matter what, He can do anything. He can make you well. Nothing's too much for Him. You keep fighting and resting in Him. I have to leave now. We don't want to tire you out. I'll be back. We're all here praying for you."

She'd left then, and had returned to the chapel to pray for his continued strength, hoping he had heard her.

Watching him now, she knew what she hadn't then. Each beat of his heart was an act of will. Because a short time ago, Gerald North, the surgeon in whom Brian had placed such faith, had given them a much less optimistic view of Greg's chances than his brother had. North was amazed that he'd been able to keep Greg alive during surgery, and that Greg had hung on through the night.

"It isn't that any one injury is so catastrophic," he'd told them. "If Greg recovers, he'll be almost as good as new. But it's an 'if.' He was already in a weakened state from his injury earlier in the year, and the body can take only so much. I don't mean to sound so pessimistic, but I also don't want to see all of you so positive that he'll pull through, only to be disappointed. Greg does have youth and general good health on the plus side of the equation, so who knows? Time will tell if his plus column can balance out the negative indicators."

One small two-letter word in the midst of the whole conversation had struck Angelica's heart with the ruthlessness of a sharp blade. *If. If* he recovers. Not *when*. No one was sure of anything. Then Greg's father grounded her in her faith once more.

"Greg has one other thing on the plus side, Doctor. He has the Lord and all our prayers. No offense, but the Lord can move mountains, and I don't think my son's through serving Him on earth yet."

And neither did Angelica. Greg's fight wasn't over by a long shot. Their prayer vigil continued. Twenty-four hours had passed and there had been no change—for better or for worse.

Exhausted, she turned away from Greg and crept back into the waiting room. Greg's parents slept on the sofa, propped up against each other. Brian, who claimed he could sleep anywhere, lay on his back on the floor under the window at the far side of the room.

Jim sat next to Joy, his sister. The tall, willowy, blond woman was a bulwark of strength, if a bit brash. But the important thing was that she seemed to know when Jim needed a break from the hospital and the disinfectant smell that set him so on edge. Unfortunately, she was asleep now, and Jim was getting restless. He stood and stalked to the window overlooking the courtyard.

Angelica approached him for the first time, drawn by his love for Greg and his deep sorrow. "Maybe you should think about going home," she said quietly.

"I tried that. He's there, too."

"And so is your Jessie?"

She saw Jim grimace, even though he stood in profile to her. "She's there. She's here. She's at The Tower. With Greg so bad—" he shook his head "—it just brought it all back, is all."

"Greg wouldn't want you here, suffering on his account. And your sister is out on her feet. Why don't you take her home and sack out on her sofa?"

Jim turned, a look of confusion and shock written on his features. "Why are you being so nice to me? I've treated you like dirt since we met."

"You were upset. And we didn't meet under the best of circumstances," Angelica explained. She tried not to think about those awful minutes, but it was no use. The memories drew her. Every time she closed her eyes, she saw the look on Jim's face when he glanced over at Greg and grabbed the phone, shouting, "Officer down!"

"Are *you* all right?" Jim asked, his arm suddenly around her. "Come on, let's sit down. You just went pale as a sheet."

"I just keep remembering. It plays itself over and over in my head. Do you ever get used to this?"

"My dad was a cop. He always said that if violence didn't touch you, it was time to get out. Of course, in my division we don't see the things that guys like Greg see every day. I'm sorry for the way I treated you yesterday. If Greg ever found out how I spoke to you, he'd blow his stack."

"I think you're probably wrong. He'd probably agree with your assessment. I was at fault."

Jim smiled. "You need to get to know Greg a little better. The only person Greg ever has trouble forgiving is himself. The rest of us are allowed to have clay feet. And I was wrong—I wasn't really thinking things through. Joy said she'd have— Well, Joy would have made your reaction to Greg's confession look mild." He grinned, his eyebrows arching.

"Joy's a little volatile. But she made me see all this from your side. You'd have calmed down. He'd never have left the mission without you two working things out. You just never got the chance. I wish I knew how they found out that Greg was a cop and was onto them. My boss is afraid we've got a leak in the department."

So much had happened that she'd never questioned why Worth was at the mission. "Where did Greg go that night?"

"I picked him up and took him to The Tower."

Angelica closed her eyes, seeing a car pull out of a spot and follow the car bearing Greg. There had been something odd about it: the lights had been off. "You were followed. It was dark but I think the car was gray or silver—a late model and kind of nice for North Riverside.''

Jim named a make and model, and Angelica nodded.

''The judge's clerk drives one of those. Thanks. I'll call this in.''

Angelica sank back into the chair and closed her eyes. She heard Jim talking to someone, but ignored the conversation until she heard him say, ''Your daughter's over there near the window, Mr. and Mrs. DeVoe.''

Chapter Sixteen

Angelica couldn't believe her ears. Then she looked up and could scarcely believe her eyes, either. Her parents—here! Her father's hair had gone completely white, but otherwise he looked unchanged by the past two years. Gaither DeVoe was still the same tall, thin, well-dressed businessman he'd always been. And her blond, blue-eyed mother, Iris, wore her middle years well. She looked elegant, as always.

Glancing at Thomasina and Bud Peterson, dozing and still holding hands, Angelica couldn't help but notice the contrasts. Greg's parents were rumpled and exhausted after twenty-four hours of upheaval and worry over their son. She remembered Greg's stories about his childhood. These people were real parents—the kind she and Tracy had always wished for.

As her parents started across the room toward her, Angelica stood, unwilling to expose the Petersons to her parents' superior attitude toward the middle class. With Greg hovering between life and death, they certainly didn't need to wake to one of Iris DeVoe's disagreeable scenes.

"We should talk somewhere else," she told her parents stiffly, and led them to the nurses' station, where she asked if there was somewhere to talk privately. The nurse nodded and sent them to a small conference room just down the hall. On the way, Angelica realized that her head had begun to pound to the rhythm of her quickened pulse.

Why did she still let them upset her? And what on earth were they doing here? She closed her eyes for a moment. No matter what they did, they were still her parents. And she still cared, even though she knew they'd only come to castigate her for once more drawing media attention.

The front page headline—Undercover Cop Shot at Mission—and its subheading—Hero Cop Saves Angel of N. Riverside—could hardly have missed their notice or that of their circle of friends. The article had even quoted a mission resident as saying that Greg and Angelica were in love.

With every step, Angelica could feel her anger grow. How could they do this to her? How could two people be so wrapped up in their own needs that they couldn't see how cruel this was? They were her parents. How could they not know how upset she must be? How could they not care?

Angelica made sure that the wide mahogany conference table stood between them before she whirled to face her parents. She didn't know why she felt the need to have the solid barrier between them, but it made her feel more confident. "I can't believe you came here!'' Her voice cracked as she struggled for control.

"We knew we wouldn't be welcome, Angelica, but we decided we had to come to talk to you,'' Gaither DeVoe replied as he closed the conference room door.

"After two years of complete and utter silence from you, Father? You had to talk to me now? *Right now* while I'm waiting to find out if the man I love is going to take another breath?'' She wiped away angry tears and continued. "Now? When I'm blaming myself because he's even *in* the hospital?''

He nodded. "I know how long it's been. We've kept up with what you've been doing. And your mother *has* spoken to you. I felt it was better for all of us if I stayed out of your way.''

"The only reason Mother called me was to harass me and to remind me of how ashamed you both are of me. Tell me, did she make the calls because you didn't care as much as she did that I was supposedly dragging the family name around in North Riverside's gutters? Or were you worried that if you made me too angry, I'd press charges against you and your brother?''

"Why I didn't contact you no longer matters. The—''

"No longer matters?'' Angelica asked in a raised voice. "To whom? I assure you, it matters to me!''

Her father straightened his shoulders and shifted uncomfortably. "Fine. I admit I worried that you would still press charges, and I was very concerned about how your activities made the family look. And I was very wrong.''

Angelica arched an eyebrow. "Excuse me? Did I

hear you admit to being wrong about something? Better be careful, Father. That could get you a headline of your own. The Great Gaither DeVoe shocks the world with admission of—''

''Angelica, we've come here to apologize,'' her mother interrupted. ''We needed to tell you how sorry we are.''

''And to give you this,'' her father added as he reached into the breast pocket of his custom-tailored suit jacket. ''I lied about the money. I never spent it. It's always been waiting for you.'' He pushed a check across the wide table.

Angelica picked it up. The numbers jumped out at her. The entire amount of the missing funds—plus interest.

Angelica stared at the check, her hands shaking. ''It was gone. I almost lost the chance to buy our building because of what you did.''

''I didn't take the money to keep us from bankruptcy.''

''No. You didn't. You couldn't even tell the truth about your reasons for stealing my legacy from Gran. You bought that stupid yacht you both spend so much of your time on these days.''

Her father took a step back, his skin growing pale. ''You don't think much of us, do you, Angelica?''

''No. I don't think much *of* you or *about* you anymore.''

''I didn't use your money for the yacht,'' he told her.

''Why should I believe you?'' Angelica sneered. ''My whole life you've lied to me whenever it suited you. You ignored both Tracy and me for years. You weren't parents. You were absentee guardians who delegated our upbringing to schools or nannies or Gran. And when you pilfered my account, it was clear that you weren't even decent guardians.''

Gaither DeVoe nodded. Did he look older than he had a minute ago? ''A fair assessment,'' he conceded. ''Tracy said much the same things. And painful as it is, I have to agree wholeheartedly with both of you. Your mother agrees as well, and we're both sorry.''

''Very sorry, dear,'' her mother added. ''That's the main reason we came here today. To apologize and to try to make up for our past mistakes. We thought you were alone here. We wanted to help if we could.''

Did they really think that she was this gullible? They were probably just afraid that with all her current police contact, she might finally decide to press charges. That had to be why they'd returned her inheritance this way. ''Don't lie to me,'' she said through gritted teeth. ''I've spent my whole life listening to lies. I'm not spending another minute—''

Angelica gasped and sank down into a nearby chair, hearing herself as if a tape were playing in her head. She had just said almost the same words that she'd said to Greg moments before he'd been shot. *''I've spent my life caring about liars. I don't intend to continue on a path of destruction, or to listen to any more lies from you. If you won't pack your things, then I will.''*

Staring down into her lap, Angelica watched her tears drop on the same spot where Greg's blood had stained her slacks. What was wrong with her? Hadn't she lamented the fact that her mother hadn't even tried to apologize for taking the money? That two years ago her father had refused to even discuss what he'd done, after telling her unapologetically that it had been necessary to save the family name? Now they were here, doing what she'd said she wanted. And she'd almost rejected their efforts out of bitterness.

Something Greg said on the Sunday night when he'd preached on love came back to her. *"If Jesus could forgive us for all the sin he bore for us on the cross, and if he could forgive each of us for our own personal sins just because we ask him to, then who are we to deny anybody forgiveness if someone asks for it?"*

"Who am I?" she asked herself aloud. She had denied Greg forgiveness and he still might die because of her anger. Now she was doing the same thing to her parents. She looked up at her parents, tears blinding her as she stared at them. "I'm so sorry," she whispered, her throat aching. "So very sorry."

Her mother came around the table then. Awkward and unpracticed though her embrace was, she wrapped her arms around her daughter for the first time in years. It felt wonderful.

"Don't cry, Angel," her father said. "We knew you were bitter when we came here. And we accepted that you had a right to your feelings. I just thank the Lord we may still have time to make amends."

Angelica looked up at her father, shock suspending her breath. He, too, had called her Angel once upon a time. She'd forgotten the man he'd been. The man who'd hoisted her on his shoulders and carried her into the waves at the Jersey shore. The man who'd let her bury him in the sand, and who'd taught her how to build a sand castle.

"What happened to us, Daddy?" she asked, tears coursing down her cheeks.

"I started following the wrong god. I worshiped at the temple of Wall Street. My idols were cars, boats, bank accounts and a six-figure income. And I led your mother right down that path with me.

"We were both so sure that we were fine, upstanding, moral, heaven-bound Christians, and that you'd become involved in some off-the-wall cult. Then we went looking for Tracy at July Jam and we realized exactly what we were. I admit the music wasn't anything we could relate to, but then Joe Conway started his message. We stopped looking for her and looked deeper into our hearts. We couldn't ignore what he had to say, and we finally saw ourselves for what we'd become. And we understood exactly what you'd been trying to tell us."

"I can't tell you how convicted we were of the sin in our lives. But it was wonderfully liberating to understand that we weren't doomed because we'd been wrong," Iris said.

Her father nodded in agreement, then went on. "We met Tracy on the floor when we went forward to accept Jesus. We'd looked through every section of that arena, trying to find her so we could save her from the fate we thought you'd suffered. We couldn't find her anywhere, yet she was the first person we saw when we stepped down onto the floor. He used her to get us there, then kept her hidden until the time was right. It turns out that she was sitting in the next section over, and she'd watched us through the whole message. It was a miracle.''

Angelica was speechless. She stared at them, noticing for the first time that her mother's mouth and eyes had a kinder, softer look about them, and that her father's high-powered arrogant aura was gone.

"We wanted to call you the next morning, but then we decided that we had a lot of thinking to do first. And a lot of forgiveness to ask of God this week.''

"This is so wonderful,'' Angelica said. "I'm so glad you came.'' She looked down at the check she'd crumpled in her hand; the ink had run from her tears. "Tell me about the money again. This time, I promise to listen.''

Her father pulled another chair out and sat in front of Angelica and her mother. "It's a simple story of misguided parents trying to protect their daughter from what they saw as foolishness. With your uncle's help, we put the money into another account. We'd hoped to save it for the day you came to your senses and abandoned the mission.

"I understand now why you'll never do that, and we'd like to help. It sounds as if you've just lost a major contributor and trustee. We'd like to replace the judge and his funds. It's about time we started giving back to God some of what He's given us, and supporting our daughter in His work.''

"With Greg so critical, I'd forgotten about Judge Whiting.''

Iris patted her hand. "We'd like it if you'd let us stay with you and Greg's parents while you wait for Greg to wake. We have a lot to thank that young man for.''

Angelica nodded. "I'd like that." She stood and held out her hands to her parents. "We need to get back, too. I spent most of last night watching him through the window while I prayed for him. The doctors are afraid we'll tire him if we're in there too much, but I can't stand to let him out of my sight for long."

They returned to find Gerald North and Brian with the Petersons. Brian was saying, "Calm down, Mom. This is a good thing. The respirator was just helping him along a little. We weren't keeping him alive with it."

"And now you think he can breathe on his own?" Bud Peterson asked, the hope in his voice a living thing.

"We know he can," Gerald North said. "He's doing very well. Better than I thought possible. We've been bringing him up out of the anesthesia slowly for hours. Taking him off the respirator is just the next step. I'd like you all to start sitting with him in rotation. Talk to him. Encourage him."

For the next four hours, Angelica and the Peterson family took turns in fifteen-minute segments. They read to him from the Psalms and talked to him. Brian was with him now; Angelica's turn was next. She stood in her customary spot at the window, just watching Greg and praying for a positive change. Footsteps behind her drew her attention. Greg's parents and her own were on their way up the hall.

"No change?" her father asked.

Tears welled up in Angelica's eyes and she shook her head. "Now I wish Dr. North hadn't been so encouraging this morning. Every minute he doesn't wake up feels like an eternity. I just want to know he'll be okay.''

Gaither DeVoe gathered her into his arms. "He's going to wake any time now, Angelica. Try not to worry so much.''

Greg heard familiar words spoken in a familiar voice. The voice came from far away, but yet the person felt close at hand. "The Lord is my light and my salvation—whom shall I fear? The Lord is the stronghold of my life, of whom shall I be afraid? When evil men advance...''

"Brian," he said, wondering why his own voice seemed less familiar.

"It's about time, big brother. We're going through Psalms a second time here. Getting shot was a pretty drastic way to get me to take the time to read the Bible again.''

Greg forced his grainy eyes open and focused on Brian, who was no longer sitting, but scribbling on a chart and checking instrument panels in the space-age room. He grinned, wondering if he looked as bad as his brother did. "Nothing's too much trouble for my little brother. But I think this came close. I feel like twenty miles of bad road.''

Brian smirked. "You look like it, too," he quipped, then glanced toward a window. "There are some people outside, waiting for you to wake the heck up.''

"Angel?''

Brian smiled. "Hold on. I'll start the parade.''

Greg followed Brian's progress across the room, then his parents rushed in the door. "Son," they said simultaneously.

He noticed how haggard they both looked. "Sorry," he croaked, his throat dry and rough.

"Here," Brian said, holding a cup of water with a straw to his mouth. Greg drank thirstily.

"There's nothing to be sorry for. In fact, there are a couple of extra people here who want to thank you," his dad said, then gestured toward a window to the hall. Greg saw a well-dressed couple with their backs to the window. They were hugging each other.

"Who're they?"

"Angelica's parents."

Greg frowned and looked back, this time noticing a third person involved in the hug. "Angel? Is she okay?"

"She'll be fine now that you're awake," his mother assured him. "Brian, can't we let Angelica and her parents in?"

"I'll tell you what—I'm going to go call Jerry North to tell him his star patient's awake. That way I can play dumb about the number of people in here. Keep up the good work, big brother," he called over his shoulder as he sauntered out.

Greg watched as Brian spoke to the DeVoes and Angel. He was surprised to see them there, and even more surprised at the affection he'd seen among the three of them. Brian strode away after a few moments, and the DeVoes moved toward the door. But Angel shook her head, waving them in. Was she still so angry that she didn't even want to see him? She'd told him everything was okay, hadn't she? Had it just been wishful thinking?

"...our son, Greg," he heard his father say. Greg dragged his gaze from Angelica, who stood alone, her back against the window. "Greg, this is Angelica's father, Gaither, and her mother, Iris."

Greg glanced again at the window where Angel stood. She looked so alone. When he looked back at her parents, he didn't know how to treat the people who had so deeply hurt the woman he loved. "Mr. and Mrs. DeVoe," he said, keeping a neutral tone. He tried to lift his hand and offer it to Angel's father, but he couldn't get it more than a couple of inches off the bed. He felt like a dishrag: limp and wrung out.

"We don't want to tire you out, but we had to take this opportunity to thank you for saving our daughter's life. If there is anything we can do for you, please let us know. I'd be only too happy to pick up your expenses until you're back on your feet."

Greg was having trouble staying focused. He was so tired. "I'll be fine. 'Sokay—the city does that." He felt his eyes begin to drift shut of their own accord. He forced them open and looked once again toward Angel. He stared, willing her to turn around.

"Greg," Thomasina said.

He dragged his gaze to his mother.

"Suppose we all get out of here and let you and Angelica have a few minutes together?"

Had his mind slowed down or something? He just couldn't seem to stay focused on anything or what anyone was saying. Him and Angel? Together. Alone. He smiled. "Oh, yeah. That'd be great. I want to see Angel, if she'll see me."

"If?" his mother asked, sounding amused.

She might think he'd said something funny, but there wasn't anything funny about how angry and hurt

Angel had been. Greg pondered that. No, nothing funny at all. Maybe he'd just close his eyes…and wait for her to come in. *If* she came in. Yeah, he'd close his eyes just for a second…or two.

Chapter Seventeen

Greg's nose twitched. The scent of angels, he decided groggily. Angels? He frowned. How would he know what an angel smelled like? He sniffed the air carefully. His mind cleared a bit and he recognized the delicate scent. It wasn't just any angel. It was *his* Angel.

Then it all came rushing in: a film in fast-forward, ruthlessly unclouding his mind. The argument with Angel, with all its harsh words and accusations. The anguish in her eyes as she looked up at him after his angry kiss. Her demand that he leave. The sound as the door to his room crashed against the wall when Angel shoved it open. The gun leveled at Angel. The terror he felt when fear for her life had gripped him. The memories all rushed back...

"It's all right, Greg. They gave you something for the pain. Sh-sh. Breathe easy. It'll ease soon," the voice of his angel assured him.

Greg could feel her as well as smell her scent. She

wiped his face, then took hold of his hand. He could have been in heaven were it not for the unmerciful pain. His eyes flew open as a spasm hit him in his belly. He gasped, sucking air with the shock of it. Too late, he realized what a colossal mistake that was, because now his chest felt as if it, too, were on fire.

"Jesus. Oh, Jesus. Make it stop," he shocked himself by crying aloud.

Then his eyes fastened on Angel, who stood over him, speaking in a soothing whisper. "Sh-sh. It'll stop in a few minutes," she promised, her green eyes fluid with tears. She glanced toward someone else. "It will, won't it?"

"He'll feel better soon. I gave it to him intravenously so it'll take hold in a couple more minutes." That was Brian's voice. "I'll leave you two alone. Don't let him get too tired."

It was hard to concentrate with so much pain bombarding him, but Greg thought he remembered being with Brian earlier and with his parents, too. But this awful pain hadn't been there then, he recalled. Maybe he'd dreamed his family's presence, because it seemed to him that Angel's parents had been there, too. And that just wasn't possible.

Greg gritted his teeth and tightened his hand around Angel's as another spasm hit. She squeezed back as if to lend him what strength she could. He waited for the torture to pass, but it didn't. How could a couple of minutes take so long? He stared up into Angel's eyes, trying to summon the strength to talk in spite of the pain it caused, because he just couldn't stand to wait any longer. "I'm sorry...I had to lie to you. Please tell me you—"

She put her fingertip to his lips and shook her head, her smile infinitely sad. "No. Don't you worry about that," she told him, tears overflowing her beautiful eyes. She blotted the track of tears with a tissue, then wiped his face, too.

Greg blinked furiously, embarrassed to realize that the moisture on his face was also tears.

"None of that is important anymore," she went on.

"I hurt you." He took a shallow breath, which didn't hurt as bad as the last one. "It's important to me. I—"

"And I didn't hurt you?" she asked, stepping on his words. "You're here like this because of me."

"No." It came out as a groan. He didn't want her to feel responsible. He'd put her in danger by working out of her mission.

"Yes! You were shot because of me," she insisted. "And I'm sorry. I should have listened, Greg. I shouldn't have let past disappointments color my whole life. I've been judgmental and unforgiving. You had a good and honorable reason for keeping me in the dark about who you were and why you were at the mission. I endangered you because of my anger. I took your mind away from the job you had to do."

"A job I hated. Right from the first second I saw you, I hated what I had to do. It always felt wrong."

She nodded. "I know that now. But, more to the point, I should have known it then. I should have known *you*. The sad part is—I did. But I was so angry that I convinced myself that *all* the things you'd said were lies."

"So many lies—my name, why I was there...it was no wonder you couldn't sort it all out. I was trapped by the job and I didn't have a way out." Greg sighed. "What good is working to right wrongs if you have to be wrong to do it?"

Angel paused. "Think about that," she whispered, "not now, but later. You made the only honorable choice open to you in this circumstance."

"I knew for weeks how it would be when you found out. I felt so guilty every time I had to tell you another lie. It haunted me."

"The way Jessie's death haunts you?" Angel asked.

Greg nodded, however reluctantly, not willing to lie to her ever again. For a long moment he stared back at her, trying to hide the depth of the guilt he felt. Right from the first, though, she'd had a way of seeing into his soul—into his sorrow.

And she had that eagle-eyed look about her now as she stood, watching for a reaction to Jessie's name. She reminded him of a cat sitting outside a mouse hole—cute, cuddly, relentless.

Angelica knew Greg's physical pain had eased. He was able to talk more easily, and his hand had relaxed in hers. His breathing had evened out, as well. But in his eyes, that other pain was still there. The load he'd carried inside himself was no lighter now that she knew the truth about him.

It would be funny if it weren't so sad. He really thought that she couldn't see what he felt, and that he could hide all that remorse and misery. She had to make him see the truth. If it was the only thing she ever did for him—the only thing she could leave him with—she had to help Greg find the peace Jesus had promised those who placed their faith and trust in Him.

"I don't want you to bear any burden over what you had to do to clean up North Riverside," Angelica told him. "So I forgive you for any lies you had to tell me. It's over. It's as if none of it ever happened."

Greg frowned and shook his head. It was exactly the reaction she'd expected.

"Am I forgiven for getting you hurt?" she asked before he could voice the protest she saw in his eyes.

"I told you. It wasn't your fault. Worth—"

"Am I forgiven?" she repeated.

He blinked. "Well, yeah. If you need to hear me say it that way. You're forgiven. Even though there's nothing to forgive," he hastened to add.

Angelica chuckled at his stubbornness—his wonderful stubbornness—and smoothed a lock of hair off his forehead. "Thank you for your forgiveness. Now that we're past that, when are you going to forgive yourself?"

The utter confusion in Greg's expression would have made her laugh were the situation not so serious. And so frustrating. He was utterly unable to excuse himself for anything. Even for things that hadn't been his fault.

"You weren't to blame for Jessie, or your brother, or Adam Jones, or the brick that hit me, or the lies you had to tell to get a dirty, necessary job done."

"You don't understand. It was—"

Exasperated, Angelica put her hand up to silence him. "I understand perfectly. You told me yourself that you abandoned the idea of going into the ministry because of your brother's death. But your brother, who made his own choice, by the way, was not your responsibility. He had parents, too, who missed his involvement in drugs. Do you blame them for his death?''

"No," he replied without hesitation, but with an abundance of confusion in his tone. Confusion that she knew had nothing to do with the drug he'd been given for pain. She moved on to his next load of guilt.

"Wasn't it Jessie who made the mistake that gave you away? Jim says it was. You couldn't have known what she'd done. Even she must not have known. And Adam Jones went looking for trouble the night he was shot, and he found it."

"I was with Jim at The Tower for a meeting. If I'd been there…"

"Since when are you supposed to be omnipresent? And all-knowing in the case of Jessie's mistake? I thought those were God's attributes."

"Okay. I couldn't be two places at once," he conceded, however grudgingly.

Angelica looked at the ceiling in exasperation. "And you couldn't have been in the mind of a criminal to know that Jessie had given you two away. You told your superior that you had a bad feeling about that night, so he brought in extra men.

"The night of the gas leak at the mission, you came home and found the leak, then you went looking for Adam—a stranger—to try to keep him out of trouble. You found him in time to lead him to the Lord and save his life. And still you feel guilty. Can't you see how destructive that is?"

Greg didn't comment. He just stared up at her, his sapphire eyes grave, his thoughts clearly in a turmoil.

"I learned something very important today that I want to tell you about," she continued in the face of his silence. "I'm hoping it will help you see how wrong you are. My parents came here."

"Then I did see them earlier." His eyes narrowed in deep thought, then widened. "And you were hugging them. I saw you through the window."

Angelica nodded and smiled a little, remembering the past hours and the support she'd felt from her mother and father. It had been a dream—a prayer— come true. "That I was. But I almost rejected them the way I rejected you. I almost sent them away without allowing them to ask for the forgiveness they needed, or to offer the comfort they came to give.

"My parents followed Tracy to July Jam last week. But it turned out much differently from the way I thought it would. They made a decision for Christ while they were there. Perhaps my greatest sin against them was that I'd given up on their salvation. And in my bitterness, I almost didn't listen to them, either. Then I heard myself tell them that I didn't intend to listen to any more lies. I couldn't get another word out. Those were almost exactly the same words I'd said to you minutes before you were shot.

"The Lord hit me right over the head with my own words. And then He reminded me of something you'd said during the message you gave at the mission. You said it's our duty to forgive others because Jesus forgives us. This time I understood, and I applied it to myself."

"I'm glad for you," he said, but he sounded tense.

Angelica didn't want to cause him stress, but she also knew that he couldn't go on making life choices based on guilt and a need to make reparation where none was required. She pushed on.

"Now I'm telling you to listen to your own words. And I'll ask you again, when are you going to forgive yourself the way He's forgiven you? Isn't it just as wrong to harbor guilt as it is to harbor transgressions? Isn't it wrong to withhold forgiveness from yourself?" She didn't add, *especially when the guilt is misplaced.* He had enough to come to grips with.

After several minutes of watching Greg ponder her words, she saw understanding dawn in his expression. He pursed his lips, then he grinned sheepishly. "You're right. I have done that, haven't I?"

But there was still sadness in his eyes. That sparkle that she loved—the one she'd seen too infrequently—was still missing. Angelica felt suddenly unsure. Was it her presence that made him look so unhappy, reminding him of possibilities now dead for him?

Maybe she'd assumed too much when he'd asked to see her. Had she killed his feelings for her? Perhaps he could forgive her, but couldn't love her anymore. She'd been so sure that he'd come to love her.

"I guess I should be leaving," she choked out.

Greg stayed silent, but his eyes—those expressive eyes—took on a desperate edge. "If you have to," he whispered, and swallowed deeply, his breathing changing to short pants. "If it's like you said. If none of it really matters anymore."

Hope bloomed in Angelica's heart. Had he misunderstood? Did he think she'd meant the feelings between them didn't matter to her anymore?

"The *lies* don't matter, Greg," she explained. "I'll cherish the rest of the memories in my heart till the day I die. You became a very important part of the mission's family. The time you spent there touched all our hearts. Your deep faith changed hearts as well as lives.''

''What about your heart? Your life?''

''Don't you know how important you are to me?''

He only stared, his eyes a bit glazed.

''Apparently not,'' she said, leaning forward to cup his cheek. She knew that if she declared her feelings, and he was only sorry to lose her friendship, her pride would take a tremendous beating. But to lose him because of foolish pride would be just plain stupid. She had to take the chance—or regret it forever. She kissed him. ''You mean so much to me, Greg. Since Gran died, no one has been there for me. No one has stepped in and taken care of me or supported me. And no one ever made me feel the things you do. I could live without you in my life, but I don't want to try.''

Greg let out a deep sigh and closed his eyes. ''Oh, that was close.'' He smiled and opened them again. They sparkled; that inner light shone like diamonds in their blue depths. ''Don't you ever scare me like that again. I thought— Oh, never mind what I thought.'' He reached up and curled his hand over the back of her neck, pulling her toward him for another kiss. ''I'm sorry that the last time I kissed you, it was in anger. It'll never happen again. I promise.''

''I was so afraid I'd lose you. Oh, Greg it was so close. You just don't know how close it was. Your heart stopped at the mission, and it took so long for the paramedics to get it going again.'' Tears flooded her eyes.

''I'm sorry you had to go through that. I love you,

sweetheart." He smiled. "That felt so good. I've wanted to say that to you for so long, but I couldn't tell you how I felt until you knew *who* was saying it."

Angelica sank to the chair by the bed and put her head on his shoulder, suddenly overwhelmed by how close they'd come to never having these precious moments.

Greg looked down at the top of Angel's head, feeling her tears wet the shoulder of his hospital gown. "Hey, don't fall apart on me now, sweetheart. We still have some important stuff to talk about. How's it going to look when we tell our grandchildren that all you did was cry when I told you I loved you?"

All he got back were sniffles. "You could say something here. I'm gettin' real nervous."

She looked up, smiling through her tears. "I love you, too. So much." Then a teasing light came into her green eyes. "Did you say *grand*children?"

He grimaced. Real smooth, Peterson, he thought. "I guess that was sort of backward, wasn't it? I should have mentioned our children first."

She rolled her eyes.

"I—ah…guess I should have mentioned the marriage part before kids, huh?"

Angel made a strangled sound and dropped her forehead down onto his arm, her shoulders shaking.

"Are you crying again?"

She looked up, all giggles and leftover tears.

"Give a guy a break, will ya? I've never done this before. And I'm not exactly in a position to get down on one knee."

Angel bit her lower lip, clearly trying to get hold of her laughter. She propped her elbow on the bed, resting her chin on her hand, and gazed at him, her face beaming with happiness. "So this is a proposal?"

Greg grinned. "Yeah. How am I doing?"

A smile bloomed on Angel's lips. "You have a novel approach, I give you that."

"I'd rather you gave me an answer," he grumbled. He was making a muck of the most important moment of their lives! Greg took a breath and tried again. "Angelica DeVoe, will you marry me? Be my love? Have my children? Grow old with me? Did I leave anything important out this time?"

"I can't hold them off any longer," Brian called as he breezed in. "Hope this is a good time."

Greg was too glad to be alive to be annoyed with his little brother at that moment. He was sure that he saw his answer—his future—in Angel's eyes. "That depends," he said, never taking his eyes off her, "on what Angel says next.... Well?"

"I'd be honored to marry you, have your children and grow old with you," she said, smiling as she stood and leaned over him to seal their promise with a kiss.

Epilogue

Six months later

Greg combed his damp, medium-length hair, then paused to stare at his reflection. He smiled, remembering a night he'd stared into the same mirror after he'd shaved off his beard and tied back his long, unruly hair. He had been floundering, unsure who he was. Now Greg knew who the man staring back at him was. He knew him, and knew where he was headed.

The day he'd made the last decision that put him on this road rose in his mind....

"What is *this* supposed to mean?" Captain Glen Harris bellowed as he rushed into Greg's hospital room.

It was a week after Greg had first awakened in confusion. It had been a week of pain, of recuperation, of happiness, and of soul-searching.

When Harris tossed a sheet of paper onto Greg's lap, he picked it up. "It's my resignation," Greg explained with exaggerated patience. "It's pretty straightforward, Captain. It says 'After a great deal of prayer and soul-searching—'"

"I know what it says. What I want to know is why."

"Because being an undercover cop isn't what the Lord would have me do with my life anymore. It may never have been. It's too late to change the past, but I can still change my future."

"You're the best officer I have."

"Was. I *was* a good officer. I did a good job, but it's one I can't do anymore."

"What does your being a cop have to do with God?"

"The Lord has *everything* to do with what I do with my life. He has a plan for each of our lives. And I've come to see that police work was never His plan for me. Who knows—maybe that's why I keep getting hurt in the line of duty. Maybe letting me get shot was his way of waking me up."

"You think God let you get shot up to make you quit? Have you got a screw loose, Peterson? If you're burned out from too much undercover work, I can understand that, but quitting is too rash a decision. You aren't even out of the hospital yet."

"Captain, I know what I'm doing."

"Look, try this idea on for size." Harris grabbed a chair and sat down, settling in for what looked to Greg like some heavy-duty negotiations. "You can be a regular narcotics detective. No more undercover. In fact, you could take a leave of absence and have a nice long rest. You have enough vacation time coming to you that you could take a couple of months with pay after your disability runs out. That'd give you eight, nine months to let your nerves settle."

Greg shook his head. "My nerves are just fine. I'm sorry if I'm leaving you shorthanded, but I won't change my mind. I'm leaving the force to go into the ministry. Angel and I are going to start a church out of the North Riverside Mission."

And they had. It had felt like the right decision from the second the idea came to him. And now, six months later, with more than two hundred adults and teens attending regularly and a flourishing Sunday school, he knew it was right!

A knock on his door drew Greg's attention. "Yeah?" he called out as he turned. The door opened. It was Angel. "Hey, sweetheart."

"Hi. Did you know my father's here?" She sounded puzzled.

Greg shook his head. "Nobody told me. Has he been waiting long?"

"I don't know. He was in my office when I got in a few minutes ago."

"Did he say what he wants?"

"He said he wants to talk to us in the conference room. And he brought a couple of men with him."

"Sounds mysterious."

"For the last week he's been acting as if he had a secret, but he just smiles every time Mother or I ask what he's up to. I think I've heard him say 'all in good time' about a hundred times. I have a feeling *this* is the time."

Greg nodded and tossed the comb on the dresser. "Guess we'd better find out." He followed Angel into the hall, then spun her into his arms. "But first, how about a good-morning kiss. I miss you so much when you're gone."

Angel laughed before he could kiss her, and said, "Gone? I don't leave you here at the mission till nearly ten at night, and I'm back by eight the next morning. How can you miss me when I'm here most of the time? And look who's complaining. It was your idea for me to move back with my family until we get married."

Greg only smiled and claimed her lips. As usual, he was lost in seconds. Whenever he held her, kissed her, his mind spun away into another realm.

It had been like this since that first kiss. Which was the chief reason he'd insisted they not both live at the mission. Both sets of parents had insisted on a large wedding that had done away with the short engagement he'd envisioned. And he needed the help of distance in the dark hours of the night, when thoughts of her haunted and tempted him.

Greg forced himself to pull his lips from hers. "It wouldn't have looked right for us to both stay here, and the lease was up on my apartment. Besides which, it gets more difficult every day that goes by to stop with one kiss." He sighed. "You'd think it would get to be old hat."

Angel leaned back in his arms and grinned up at him. "I don't think that was the Lord's plan when he created Eve for Adam and told them to be fruitful and multiply."

Greg chuckled and gave her another quick kiss. "I

hadn't thought of it that way. Thank heaven the wedding's only a month away.''

"Thank heaven," she agreed, her eyes dazed and alive at the same time. "My father's waiting," she said, suddenly remembering.

Greg blinked. "Your father. Right! Let's see what he has up his sleeve."

An hour later, Greg and Angel were still in a mild state of shock. Gaither DeVoe had convinced the owners of a newly formed conglomerate to settle their new plant in North Riverside. Green Thumb was the product of a merger of a prosperous lawn-and-garden hand tool company and a lawn-and-garden equipment company. This was no fly-by-night concern. They would be a major presence in North Riverside for years to come.

The owners wanted the new plant to benefit a community, not just to add to an already healthy tax base. North Riverside had a riverfront facility that was a perfect site for the new Green Thumb factory. There would be more than a thousand jobs opening up, and a job training program for locals. Grants had been promised for education and day care, and funds would be donated to Homes for Restoration to benefit employees.

Angelica's dream of a better life for the people of North Riverside had blossomed and flourished. And Greg's assignment—though it had turned out to be a trial and a test for him—had paved the way to a better life for many.

Greg's message two days later was inspired by the good news they'd gotten about the Green Thumb factory, and by the stiff sentences received by Harold

Whiting and the officers who had pled guilty rather than face trial.

"Proverbs 11:10 says, 'When the righteous prosper, the city rejoices; when the wicked perish there are shouts of joy,'" Greg quoted when he stepped forward to give that week's message. "Now I know a lot of you felt that way when the men who'd come into your midst and betrayed your trust were sentenced this week. And that's only human. But remember what Jesus said in Matthew 6:14: 'For if you forgive men when they sin against you, your heavenly Father will also forgive you.' It's our duty to forgive these men. We shouldn't wait to feel forgiveness. We need to decide to forgive, and feelings of forgiveness will follow. Because forgiveness is an act of will, not a feeling."

Angelica's heart swelled with joy. Her love for Greg and his for her had healed every sore and empty spot in her heart, just as Jesus had healed her soul. With the Lord's certain help, their love would last forever.

* * * * *

Dear Reader,

Never Lie to an Angel is a story about forgiveness.
It is a mistake to wait until we feel like forgiving
someone. We must *decide* to forgive our transgressors.
For it is only after we forgive that we can move on with
our lives.

Angelica had good reason to resent her parents, but it
didn't make her feel better to harbor those feelings. It
got in the way of her development as a Christian and
caused her to be unforgiving. It hardened her heart so
that when presented with Greg's lie and his sincere
apology, she could no longer see past familiar feelings
of betrayal or her usual reaction to it. Her decision to
forgive her parents, on the other hand, opened up a new
relationship with them and greatly rewarded her.

Greg was another case altogether. He harbored guilt
and forgot the lessons of his childhood. The Lord
doesn't harbor anger but freely grants forgiveness. Greg
forgot to accept that forgiveness and to forgive himself,
which led him down a path that wasn't meant for him.
It was only when he followed the Lord's leading that he
was able to do the most good for the people he was
trying so hard to help.

I hope both Angelica and Greg have shown the value of
forgiving and accepting forgiveness. And how our lives
will be happier and more fulfilled for it.

God bless,

Kate Welsh